Max Conquers the Cosmos

Max Conquers the Cosmos

Mark Bouton

Five Star • Waterville, Maine

First Edition
First Printing: December 2003

Published in 2003 in conjunction with Tekno Books and Ed Gorman.

Set in 11 pt. Plantin by Ramona Watson.

Printed in the United States on permanent paper.

Library of Congress Cataloging-in-Publication Data

Bouton, Mark.
 Max conquers the cosmos / Mark Bouton.
  1st ed.
  Waterville, ME : Five Star, 2003.
  p. cm.
  ISBN 1-59414-072-3 (hc : alk. paper)
  1. Private investigators—Fiction. 2. Contractors—Crimes against—Fiction. 3. Rich people—Crimes against—Fiction. 4. Widows—Fiction. 5. Mystery fiction. I. Title.
 PS3602.O894M39 2003   2003060715

This book is dedicated to Floyd Bouton, my dad, who instilled in me a love of the written word.

Acknowledgments

Many thanks go to the following people for their assistance, expertise, patience, guidance, and encouragement: My family, Ellen Byers Bouton, Robert Bouton, Scott, Chad, Benny, and Dan Bouton; my writers' group, Bill Burns, Karen Barron, Kristi Pelton, Olivia Harris, Eleanor Bell, Karen Brown, and Alice Dewdney; my friends and readers, Skip and Peggy Snyder, Jean Deighton, Darrell Breider, Bobbye Straight, Ed Corcoran, Mike Powell, Jan Heath, Carol Rieger, Laura Straus, Janet Coulon, and Lavonne Carpenter; my art coordinator, Blake Zachritz; my publicity advisor, Mary Loftus; my editor, Pat Estrada; John Helfers, Acquisitions Editor at Tekno Books; and my agent, Nancy Ellis of LitWest Group, Inc.

Chapter 1

"Do you miss the sight of blood?" Bagley asks, thumbing at a gory scene that's lit up like Christmas.

"I'm aces without it," I say. "And I'll bet the dead guy's not even my type."

He snorts. "Max, you got a warped sense of humor."

"It's the best way I know to cope with death and detectives."

Bagley shakes his head, then hitches his slacks, which promptly sag from the press of his belly and a bulky .45. The shield on his belt glints under the spotlights' glare. A uniform paces up and talks low in his ear, so I check out the show.

Yellow tape circles the pool. Bright sunken lights cast an aqua glow over the cops. A sharp flash reflects off the bloody corpse.

"You're analyzing," Bagley says. "Just habit, or is it business?"

"Both. Amy Harrington called and said she'd been hired as the wife's attorney. Amy asked me to assess the case—straight PI work."

"You didn't see enough killings when you worked in the FBI?"

"Plenty, but I'm repaying a favor."

"Umm." He pulls out a cigar and rolls it between his fingers.

I study the lavish hilltop home. "Real cozy bungalow."

He bites off the tip. "Yep, it's a big ticket item. Sometimes rich guys get wasted, just like losers. It keeps life democratic."

"God bless America." I tilt my head toward the carnage. "So, what's your take?"

He lights up, pockets the match, and shrugs beefy shoulders. "The lady offed her hubby. Shot him point blank, head and chest."

"She's got no alibi?"

"A prowler did the deed, then vanished into the night."

"Anyone else see the guy?"

He exhales a dense cloud. "Who?"

"You know, the prowler."

"Hell, no. Just like no one ever sees The Shadow."

"But he's a fictional figure."

"C'mon, Max, what's your point?"

Grinning, I say, "Careful, Jeff, cynics get ulcers, you know."

"Long as I last two years, three months, and six days."

"Your retirement date?"

"Bingo."

"After which you'll be sipping wine coolers in Tahiti?"

"More like swiggin' suds in my Midwestern backyard."

I look at the body. Gray hair, ashen face, dark red rivulets branching down his forehead. "Any reason the wife would do it?"

"I dunno . . . say she hated him, or she loved him. Maybe they fought. Hey, men are from Pluto and women from Mercury."

"Right solar system, Jeff. So he's rich, is she good-looking?"

"Just like the song. Morrie was a contractor in Chicago, but he moved here to Hillsboro two years ago. She's younger, a real babe."

"What's her status?"

"She's got blood on her blouse, trace metals and residue on her hands. Said she fired at the phantom prowler as he ran off. Then she tried to rouse the dead. It was messy. And unsuccessful."

"Any GSR on the vic's hands?"

"Poor Morrie? Trace metals, but no residue. It's no suicide."

So I thought. No soot on his shirt, no powder tattooing on his chest or forehead. The shots were fired from more than two feet away. He held the gun, picking up trace metals, but he never shot it.

"You going to book her?" I ask.

He rolls his eyes. "Our new Assistant D.A., the friggin' rookie, wants to wait for the autopsy."

"So, do you mind if I look around?"

"Hell, Max, why should I have all the fun?"

"I'm glad you still enjoy your work."

"I'd prob'ly pee my pants if it wasn't for my enlarged prostate."

Even with light bars glaring, it's hard to spot details out here. The wife's too wired to question now, but she doesn't look goofy enough to shoot someone. Still, passion can make fools of us all.

I examine the corpse, take pictures. A dead body projects a terrible finality. And murder defines our species as grimly primal.

Detective Bill Wahr stands twenty feet away, examining a Colt Python. It's a striking gun, and deadly. He opens the cylinder.

"Fully loaded?" I ask.

"Hey, Max Austin. I didn't notice you there. Is this one of those *Time* magazine federal cases?"

Wahr is a tall drink of water, originally from New Jersey,

11

with a loud, nasal voice. He's always quick with a quip.

"It's PI work, Bill. I gave up the fancy government perks."

"And you had it so cushy." He ejects the cylinder's contents, then holds out a gloved hand. "Big bad Python was chock full of .357 copper-jacketed cartridges. Three intact, three fired. Two stopped by our guest of honor."

"Anyone find the third round?"

"No, not yet. I'd guess maybe never."

Looking around, I see that everyone's doing their routine, but there's no urgency or intensity. I'll bet they think it's a slam-dunk. Maybe it is.

It's getting late when I steer my Expedition up the gravel drive to my farmhouse perched on a hill. Soft lights from town, ten miles away, smear the horizon. Binga lumbers off the porch to greet me, and I stroke her thick coat, saying, "How's my good girl doing?"

Inside, I spoon huge chunks of canned food into a bowl, which Binga downs in three gulps. "Jeez, take a breath, girl." I snag a beer to filter my thinking and grab a dog biscuit for Binga's dessert. A glob of black hair the size of a tumbleweed graces the white tile kitchen floor, and I kick it toward the trash. German shepherds.

Shrugging off my blazer, I toss it on a chair. My RocSports squeak as I hobble across the hardwood floor toward the living room. Binga trails me, her toenails clicking until she reaches the Turkish rug.

I switch on lights, then lob the biscuit, which Binga grabs on the fly. She flops on her mat beside the sofa to gnaw the goody into crumbs. My leather chair absorbs me like a cloud, and I deflate, then pop the top on my can of solace.

From its spot in the bay window, my telescope beckons, but right now I'm absorbed in this case. I do like to search out small secrets of the universe, just as I sought glimpses of truth in the FBI. Likely, I'll never fully understand the cosmos, just as no case is ever wholly solved, every relationship identified, all motives known.

A question streaks through my brain like a cosmic particle: Did Mrs. Jacobsen whack her old man? Conditions indicate she did. But we clever humans once thought the sun revolved around the Earth.

I ponder the cosmos because it's the biggest mystery of all. Whodunit, howdunit, and whydunit; inquiring minds want to know. Why are we here, and do other intelligent beings share our universe?

Astronomers know of other planets that might support life, but none with a Web site. And even though the waves/particles zip along at six trillion miles a year, some light takes billions of years to reach the Earth. Many of the stars that sent it could be dead.

Einstein noted an interesting oddity: light curves as it passes through the intense gravity of massive objects. And . . . "Oh, shit."

The bending of light reminds me of something. Limping to my jacket, I pull out the photos from the pool. As I flip through them, I stop to examine one.

"Ah, I thought so," I say. The principles of physics always apply. Something besides gravity made Morrie's wrist bend at that angle.

Binga's snoring wakes me. "Thanks, girl," I say, but the din continues. Time to rise, anyway, there's detective work to be done.

I nix the alarm, then glance at the photo on the night

table of Sharon and me at the beach on South Padre Island. With a T-shirt, I wipe the picture glass. Life out here is a constant battle against dust. Stroking the smooth frame, I say, "Dear, I'm off to solve a riddle."

We still have conversations in my head, though she died of cancer a year ago. I suppose it's much like losing an arm or leg. Supposedly, people can still feel an ache or an itch in the missing limb. Indeed, my memories, like phantoms, seem to haunt this house. I replace the picture in its spot.

Binga rouses herself, acting hungry, and we head downstairs.

"Morris Jacobsen," says the newsman on my kitchen TV, "was planning to build a large industrial park east of town." He adds that the contractor had previously built such parks in Dallas and Chicago. "No arrests have been made, and police continue to investigate."

Outside, I squint against arrows of morning sun while Binga pees. Fall has wafted in like a leaf. Morrie was into the autumn of his life, as am I, but he never got to fully enjoy the colorful, poignant season—bullets in the head and chest.

Hillsboro has fine folks, decent schools, superb fast food. "But," I say aloud, "why did Morrie and his wife come here?" He'd done well in large cities, then he moved to this small town. What if she was unhappy here, and he wouldn't leave? Would she get desperate?

Once more, I wind my way up into the Clarion subdivision. It's a staged neighborhood that rambles across a hilltop suited for looking down on others. People pay big bucks to live in these houses featuring yards like pool table felt, beds of planted flowers that look artificial, and stain-free circular drives for posing pricey cars.

At the apex of all this high living stands Vickie Jacobsen's stucco-sided abode, capped with a ton of red

Spanish tile. It exudes the aura of a fortress, minus only a few cannons. The retaining walls, made of monster slabs of granite, almost make the hill sag.

After I ring the bell, Mrs. Jacobsen opens it and I introduce myself. "Come in," she says, smiling with perfect white teeth. Her face is striking, her skin creamy and radiant. She exudes an aroma of expensive perfume. "Call me Vickie," she says. Okay, I'll try.

An overstuffed chair in the vast living room beckons to me. Seated in comfort, I gaze through a huge picture window to watch the sun spreading across the poorer sections of town. Vickie's wearing shorts, her muscled legs curled under her on the sofa. Her champagne blond hair is cut like a model's. She's flat out gorgeous.

Taking out my notepad, I say, "All right, Mrs. . . . um, Vickie, can you tell me what happened here last night?"

"I already told the police."

"But I like to ask my own questions."

"My story isn't going to change."

"Perhaps you'll recall more details."

She sniffs impatiently. "So here we go again. As I said, Morrie and I were about to go to bed. He thought he heard a noise outside. I told him to forget it, but he got his gun and went out there."

"Did you see what happened?"

"I went upstairs. I was brushing my teeth when I heard shots."

"How many?"

"Two. I ran downstairs, looked out the patio door, and saw Morrie lying beside the pool. A man was at the fence, climbing out."

"Could you see the man's face?"

"Only his back."

"Could you describe him?"

"He was tall. About your height, actually, but a little heavier. He was wearing slacks and a sports shirt."

"Did you call 9-1-1?"

"I ran outside to Morrie. He lay there totally still. I picked up the gun and shot at the man, then I tried to revive Morrie."

"You just took one shot?"

"The man was into the trees. I could barely see him."

"Have you fired that revolver before?"

"I've shot it some."

"Can you hit anything with it?"

"Yes, I'm familiar with firearms. My dad was in the military. He taught me and my sister to shoot."

Closing my notepad, I say, "All right, that's all for now."

"Fine." She checks her watch.

"Do you have another appointment?"

"No, I'm just going to the club to hit some practice serves."

That catches me by surprise. "Vickie . . . I'm not your attorney, but I think it would probably look better if you stay home and play the role of the grieving widow."

She sighs; her shoulders droop. "Okay, Max, I guess you could say this has been traumatic, but I'm not grief-stricken. Just so you know, Morrie had been seeing other women. I told him I wouldn't put up with it, but he didn't stop. I'd seen a lawyer to file for divorce."

"Still, appearances could count if you ever sit facing a jury."

"I understand, but exercise helps me fight stress. Besides, why should I be charged with anything?"

"When are you meeting with Amy Harrington?"

"This afternoon. She said to ask you to come, too. Or

you could join me at the club, then we'll have lunch."

"I used to love tennis."

"You don't play anymore?"

I see my car sliding on the icy road toward the column of the overpass. With the spinal cord injury comes a numb leg and a limp. "I've decided golf is more my speed."

"Maybe I can get you interested again." She uncoils, tugs at her shorts, and crosses the carpet to a tennis bag with racquets jutting out. She leans down to pick it up, then turns to catch me watching.

"You never answered me," she says.

"About being interested?"

"No, about why I should be charged with anything."

"Because murders are often done by people who knew the victim, especially intimately. You had blood on your blouse and residue on your hands. Plus, he was shot with a gun from your bedroom."

"Actually, it was from *his* bedroom."

"After he heard a noise outside."

"Which was probably the prowler. And the killer, it turns out."

We seem to be in a never-ending orbit.

As I say goodbye, Vickie smoothes her perfect hair, and I think of Sharon's ash brown locks, often tousled, with wisps swirling away beside her smiling face. Sharon was happy and comfortable with our rural life. But I doubt that Vickie could be a country person; you get your clothes dirty, your hands cut, and your hair mussed.

Driving toward town, I tap the wheel in time to the song that requests a piña colada for each hand. Sounds like a fine idea. I check the Dow Jones average on the sign at 26th, then whiz past some of the splendid commercial ventures which keep Hillsboro humming, such as Hardee's, Toys Я Us, and Chuck E. Cheese.

The Expedition slides into a spot in front of the Sheriff's Office and Police Department, a low beige brick building. At the desk I ask for Detective Bagley. A girl with stringy red hair and pimples tells me he'll be right out, then returns to studying her *Glamour* magazine.

Bagley steps out through the security doors, sporting a houndstooth jacket. He motions me to follow. As we walk down the hall toward the squad room, he says, "You talk with the widow yet?"

"Just finished."

"Any revelations?"

I tell him there were none, but that I'd keep him posted. It's best to cooperate with the cops. They can help or hurt a PI.

As we enter the squad room, other detectives look up, smile or wave, then go back to their phones or computers.

"Hey, the fed is back," says Bill Wahr. "You find that prowler?"

"Nope, I'm still a PI, and he's still on the loose."

"Why am I not surprised?"

In a large cubicle, Wahr and I flop onto old wooden chairs facing Bagley's outsized metal desk. Piles of papers assume a semblance of order, with his IN box much fuller than the OUT. Personal photos and mementos are relegated to a credenza behind his padded office chair.

Wahr gives me a cool stare. "You carrying?"

"Reckon so, partner."

"What, that 10 mm?"

"That was the Bureau's. I've got a .357."

"Do you still pack all those crazy weapons?"

"What do you mean?"

"The 'pen' that's a gun, the knife belt buckle, brass knucks."

"Hardly ever." What does he care?

Bagley has his big hands clasped on the desk. He studies me, his eyebrows wrinkly. "So, what do you need from us?"

"Whatever you've got. Officers' Reports, the coroner's."

"No coroner's yet, and the Captain's pissed about info leaking—to the press, whatever. I can't give you *carte blanche*."

Wahr leans in. "You're on the wrong side, here, Max. Tryin' to find stuff not done by the book and get a solid case bounced."

"No way. I'm after evidence, just like you guys. But there's no use us doing the same things twice."

They exchange a glance.

"Anything you find," Wahr says, "you'll show us right away?"

"What I get, you get."

Wahr stares at the cubicle wall, scowling.

Bagley gnaws his lip, then grabs a folder, stands, and walks out of the enclosure. "C'mon," he says, and I trail behind like a duckling.

At a copy machine, Bagley loads Officers' Reports, an evidence sheet, and some photos. He pokes the number two. "I need a copy of the file, but I also need a smoke real bad. Would you watch the machine to make sure it don't catch fire or somethin'?"

He leaves. The copier whirs. No fires erupt.

When the machine stops, I slip a copy into my jacket pocket. The room feels close, and I'm sweating, but not from doing something taboo. One of the photos I saw has my heart galloping.

Chapter 2

There's some time before the meeting in Amy's office, so I'll review the police files. I pull into Gage Park and stop beneath a shade tree. As I saunter toward the tattered rose garden, a squirrel claws its way up the trunk of a giant oak, a phalanx of geese honks above, and a woolly caterpillar inches along the rough bark of an ash tree.

I plop on a park bench and zip open my binder. Let's see . . . patrol officers responded to a 9-1-1 call from a neighbor. Morrie's body found beside his pool . . . shot in the chest and forehead . . . Colt Python lying nearby . . . called for backup . . . detectives dispatched.

Vickie tested positive for firing a weapon, said she shot at a prowler. Blood on her blouse. But was it because she checked on her husband, or because it was splattered when she fired the shots?

Morrie won't be chasing any more skirts. And the lady sure had blood on her hands. This scenario reads like a Shakespearean tragedy.

Indeed, the Bard said: "Nothing in his life became him like the leaving it." Might've been so for Morrie. But Vickie didn't find him *in flagrante delicto* with a floozy, so she can't claim overriding passion made her lose control. Besides, she's stuck with the prowler story.

Murder cases can be strange. Like *Dial M for Murder*, where the key switches around like magic. I hope this case isn't that baffling.

★ ★ ★ ★ ★

Amy Harrington's name and two others are imprinted on the door of a squat brown building. She's practiced in Hillsboro for fifteen years, handling criminal defense cases. She's articulate and shrewd.

The waiting room is furnished in deep cushioned chairs. I approach a curved desk and introduce myself to the receptionist, a young blond woman with vast blue eyes.

"Yes, Mr. Austin, go right on back. Second office on the left."

A thick pewter gray carpet leads to an oak-paneled door. It's open, and I rap on the door jamb, peeking inside. Amy looks up from some papers on her large oak desk, brushes her bangs aside, and smiles. She has chestnut eyes set in a porcelain face.

"Glad you could come," she says, rising from her chair and sticking out her hand. Nice manicure. Firm, warm grip.

"Good to be working with you," I say.

We sit, stare at each other for a couple of seconds too long, and her milky complexion pinkens. She shuffles some papers, then glances toward the doorway. "Our client should be here soon."

"Maybe she went into extra innings," I say. I mention Vickie's tennis practice. Amy seems taken aback by the thought of her client smacking tennis balls a day after possibly whacking her husband.

"What did you see at the crime scene?" Amy asks.

I tell her, not bringing up the wrist, which is a speculation. "And here are the police reports," I say, also not mentioning the photo of Morrie's chest, another theory I'm working on. "No coroner's yet."

She dons rimless glasses to read the reports. Intense eyes dart back and forth as she skims the material. Her hair is

21

thick, raven black, with sparse silver threads, and cut in a short bob.

"Damn," she mutters. "This could be real—"

"I hope I'm not late," Vickie Jacobsen says from the doorway.

"No, no," says Amy. "Do come in. I'm Amy Harrington." They size each other up in the way women do, which gives me a chill.

"You know Mr. Austin, of course," Amy says.

"Yes, Max and I met," Vickie says, smiling.

Amy raises an eyebrow just a centimeter.

Vickie sits down, crosses her legs, and tugs at her short skirt. We survey the effect. I don't think the tennis hurt her any.

"Max and I," Amy says, cutting me a look, "were discussing this tragic situation. And let me say, I'm very sorry for your loss."

"Thank you." No search for a hanky in her Gucci purse.

"Max got the police reports, and we'll go over them." She takes off her glasses and fixes Vickie with a stare. "But first I want you to tell me everything that happened. Every detail you can remember."

Vickie grimaces. But she tells it again. And adds a new wrinkle.

"Then I walked halfway down the stairs, and I could hear voices."

My head jerks up. There was nothing in the police reports about that. She didn't mention it to me, either.

"How many people?" I say. "And did you tell that to the cops?"

"Just Morrie and another man. You mean, about the voices?"

"Yes, the voices."

"I believe I . . . no, I . . . I'm not really sure."

Amy says, "Did you hear what was said?"

"Just a couple of muffled exchanges. But they got quiet, so I went back up to brush my teeth. Then in a minute, I heard shots."

"Were they arguing?" Amy asks.

"I don't think so, but Morrie's voice *was* loud."

"Was the other man loud, too?" I ask.

"No, it was more controlled. Sort of deep and authoritative."

"Mrs. Jacobsen," Amy says, "you heard your husband talking to a man before he was shot, and you didn't tell the police? I can't—"

"I told them I saw a man running away. I don't know if I mentioned the voices. Besides, I didn't hear what they said." She sniffs, then adds, "When I talked to the police, I was distraught, for God's sake. Morrie had just been shot."

She's as stiff as a heron, trying to convince a doubtful Amy, but I'm mollified about the case.

Vickie relates the rest of the story. It's about as written in the police report. I don't know why her mentioning the voices makes me believe her, but it sounded as though she were telling the truth. She still could have taken the gun by force or guile, plugged Morrie at close range, then told the same story. But to set up an alibi, she would've told the cops about the voices. Probably.

She said Morrie's voice was loud. The other man was calm, in control. But Morrie had the gun. If the guy had been a prowler, Morrie would've scared him off or shot him. The man wouldn't have spoken calmly, he'd have cut and run, or jumped Morrie for the gun.

The gun. Like the key in *Dial M for Murder*. Tricky.

"Was your husband comfortable shooting that revolver?" I ask.

"Morrie?" She rolls her eyes. "He liked to show it off to people, but he couldn't hit a trash can from ten feet away."

So maybe he wouldn't have shot until too late because he wasn't handy with the gun. Or maybe he knew his assailant, and he didn't expect the guy to grab the pistol and do him. Of course, you don't easily yank a gun away from someone who's holding it on you.

Which goes back to Vickie getting the gun and doing the deed. Unless I can figure out how the killer got Morrie's revolver, Vickie's got problems. At the doorway, Amy's saying she'll keep in touch.

I say, "Could I come by your house again and look around?"

"Sure," Vickie says, "feel free. I'll be there all afternoon."

She leaves, Amy turns back, closes the door, and strides toward her desk. "She's in big trouble," she says.

We dissect the case. The clues implicating Vickie don't seem to change. Later, we sit in silence. Amy drums her nails on her desk, lost in thought. She's a beauty, now that I can study her without her piercing eyes on me. Maybe I'll lose that ten pounds and—

"What're you staring at?" she says.

When did women become so direct? But I can fight fire with fire. "Your hooters, of course."

"I'll bet you were checking out my butt at the door."

"Counselor, if you don't want to be thought a hottie, you shouldn't dress like you came off the cover of *Cosmo*."

"How old are you?"

That was not a graceful segue. "Let me wait awhile before I tell you that." It'll give me a chance to grab some hair dye.

"That's okay, I don't think I'll tell you, either."

"But you have nothing to worry about."

She stares at me as though I were naked. "Neither do you."

Her desk phone rings. "Yes?" She jots something down. "Thanks, Jennifer, good work."

Hanging up, she says, "And then there's the insurance."

"How much?"

"Vickie took out a two-million-dollar term policy three months ago."

Two million more reasons she may have done it.

On the road to Vickie's, it occurs to me that if she didn't pull the trigger, then why was Morrie killed? Burglars burgle. Peeping Toms peek. Killers kill. A prowler doesn't fit the bill as a murderer.

Driving past Wal-Mart, Barnes & Noble, and West Ridge Mall, I question how Hillsboro supports all this retail business. And I wonder how anyone could fill an industrial park miles outside the city as Morrie planned. The economic potential doesn't seem to be there.

Vickie's Gothic mansion looms ahead. She answers the door wearing a thin white cover-up over a Day-Glo orange bikini. Though she looks stunning, I act cool . . . I think.

"I was sitting out by the pool," she says. "Come join me."

We pass through the living room into a den and out sliding glass doors to the sundeck. With no corpse lying there, it's a beautiful setting. Fiery sugar maples, bright yellow American elms, and glowing purple Chinese elms encircle the pool.

"There's coffee," she says. "A special blend I think you'll like."

We sit in two white wrought iron chairs at a glass top table, a yellow umbrella canted above. She pours me a steaming cup. The pool's bluer than the Hope diamond cut with a million sun sparkles.

A wisp of golden hair falls across her eye. She looks like a beautiful actress whose name I can't recall. The coffee is reminiscent of chocolate, smoked almonds, and cognac.

I say, "What will you do now?"

She gets a vacant look. "I'm not sure. But I'm certain I'll move out of this house."

"Do you have family around here?"

"A sister in Tulsa. But with two kids, a husband, and a country club life, she has no time to take care of me. I have friends who'll see me through. Some here, a few in Chicago, several in Las Vegas."

"Vegas?"

"I grew up in Las Vegas," she says. "I wasn't a showgirl or a dealer, just a civilian. It's a normal town when you get off the Strip."

"I'm sure. You just surprised me. In fact, I have friends there."

"Everyone says that. Like 'Some of my best friends are . . .' "

"Sorry, I didn't mean it to sound that way." I nervously finger the metal pole in the middle of the table.

"Be careful with that."

"Pardon?"

"The button that makes the umbrella tilt is sensitive. I don't want you to push it and get smacked in the eye."

I glance at the yellow canopy, which could bonk you a good one, all right. One last gulp of coffee. "I guess I'd better look around."

"Have at it. I'll peek out in a while."

I watch her sway back to the house, then glance around the pool. It's also first-rate. The deck is quality wood, tightly-fitted.

I examine where the body lay, trying to imagine what Morrie would have seen from this spot. To the right of the pool a wide deck abuts the water's edge, with four chaise lounges laid out side-by-side. At the far end there's a shed, probably for chemicals and equipment.

Ambling that way, I note the shrubbery is thick, tall, and still green. There's a low border of marigolds, chrysanthemums, and asters, plus leafy ground cover. All remain healthy due to a warm fall.

Wait . . . sun glints off a silvery item lying in the flowers at the foot of the bushes. I pick my way toward it, trampling sprigs and petals as I go. Ah, there it is. I pull out my Minolta for some shots.

With a handkerchief, I pick up the four-foot-long aluminum pole. It's clean; hasn't been here long. Dented four inches from the tip.

Tiptoeing out of the flower bed, I move toward the shed. It's not locked, and I pull open the door. Inside is algae remover, chlorine, and assorted rafts, beach balls, and other floatie-type objects.

Also two sections of tubing like the one I'm holding, one with a scoop net. More photos, and I think of the noise Morrie heard. Maybe the guy grabbed the tubing and knocked something over in the dark.

But why would he want a section of pole? To break a window of the house to get in? Surely he realized there was someone inside, unless he hadn't yet gotten close enough to learn that.

So if there really was a burglar, how'd he get into the pool area? I check greenery at the back. It looks solid, but I brush sections aside, peering through to the heavy-gauge fencing; now I see it.

The sharp ends at the top of a section of fence are bent down, making a spot where someone clambered over. To do what? Burgle, murder, something else? That, as the Bard would say, is the question.

Pulling a pen light from my jacket, I shine it across the ground next to the fence. The earth's soft from a rain last week. In a bare patch of dirt, there appears to be a shoe print. But maybe this is like the infamous "canals" on Mars. I'm seeing what I want to see, what would be the most exciting. Or could be it's from some voyeur.

But it looks fresh, and I wonder if it might not be connected to the prowler/killer. Also, there's a cigarette butt nearby. I recall no smell of tobacco in the house and no ashtrays on the tables.

So the guy has a smoke, breaks into the pool area, grabs a pole. Later he shoots Morrie, probably after a quarrel, because if the guy had come there meaning to snuff Morrie, he would've brought his own piece. The killing was more like a random collision of asteroids.

Then he had to run. Would he go over the fence at this same place? No, I think he would've headed for the quickest way out.

On the other side of the pool, I spot crushed flowers and a broken shrubbery limb. The fence prongs aren't bent down, and there's a gray thread stuck in them. Nice material.

Seeing nothing else, I pull out my phone.

"Jeez, Max," Bagley says, "I knew you'd cause me extra work."

"Should I watch for you sometime this week?"

He hesitates, maybe checking for stogies. "Be there in fifteen."

Opening a side gate, I meander around the fence for a closer look at the footprint. Why didn't the prowler use the gate? Maybe he didn't see it. No lock on it; I'd assume he didn't know about it.

I hunker down to study the footprint. It's a good impression, about a three-quarters shoe print, including the heel and part of the sole. Not from a boot. No tennis shoe tread, for sure. It's a man's dress shoe, size eleven or twelve. And a deep print—guy's, heavy.

More pics. I pull out a plastic bag and put the cigarette butt inside, labeling the bag. The butt's a king size Marlboro, filter tip.

"What are you doing?" Vickie says from behind me.

I jerk as if I'd had a spasm. "Where did you come from?" I say.

She just rolls her eyes.

"You surprised me," I say. "I was concentrating, considering possibilities, you know, thinking through potential evidence and . . . hey, you can jump in here anytime, say anything, stop my prattling."

"Okay, what are you doing?"

This conversation seems like a closed universe. "Collecting evidence. Taking photos. Here, kneel down." She does. "See the footprint? It could be from the guy who shot Morrie."

She gives a quizzical look, then shrugs. I'm losing my confidence again. Is this a state of utter chaos, or what?

"Did Morrie smoke cigarettes?" I ask.

She looks perplexed. "Not as long as I've known him."

"How about you?"

"Smoke makes me sneeze. Why the interest in health habits?"

"There was a butt by the footprint. Do you know anyone who smokes Marlboros?"

"I don't pay attention, but a guest wouldn't be out there."

"Could you show me where you saw the prowler leaving?"

She does; it's within a few feet of where the thread was stuck on the fence prongs. That's consistent, like planetary orbits. I take a couple of snapshots and stick the thread in another plastic bag.

Now a car drives up. Vickie lets Bagley in through the side gate, and he strides across the deck. With his hands on his hips, his Colt .45 protruding, he says, "What are you doing?"

Some days I wonder. I explain what I've found, then we both look around some more. We still can't find the bullet Vickie fired.

"Maybe she hit the guy," I speculate.

Bagley sneers, saying, "Yeah, right." Then he takes some photos and makes a cast of the shoeprint.

I ask Vickie about the pole. She doesn't know why it was in the flower bed. Bagley takes all the stuff and tags it as evidence.

Away from Vickie, I ask him, "Think this supports her story?"

He shrugs and says, "I suppose. A little."

"You know, the FBI lab might be able to tell you what kind of shoes those are from the print. Maybe get DNA from the cigarette."

"If it'd mean anything. Especially in the next two years."

"Jeff, your sights are set on the horizon. But when you view things through there, you get distortion. The atmosphere is thicker."

"Like the hot gas you're spouting?"

"No, that's what creates the stars."

As he drives off, Vickie asks, "What good is a shoe print?"

"They're sort of like fingerprints. Size, style, different wear marks on the soles—stuff like that—can be used to make a match."

"Does that ever happen in real life?"

"I've made a few cases that way. Juries love physical evidence. Makes them feel they're in the scientific age of crime detection."

"What if the man throws the shoes away?" she asks.

"Then we're out of luck. But that almost never happens."

"You're saying men are different from women?"

"In so many ways."

"A double entendre. That's cute from an older man."

Why didn't she just push me into the swimming pool? "Anyway, I need to identify this mystery man."

"Don't you think he was just some prowler?"

"No, with the talking you heard, and with Morrie not shooting him or keeping him at a distance, I think it was someone he knew."

"You mean a friend?"

"Or a business acquaintance, whatever."

"Morrie was a real estate developer. He talked to hundreds, maybe thousands of people on business."

"But it's a place to start. I want you to write down Morrie's business associates, friends, and golfing buddies. And don't forget, this could be a case of jealousy. That would mean more names."

"I don't think so." She sighs.

"Why do you say that?"

"He did fool around, but he loved me. He wouldn't get involved with anyone. He only chased women for the quick thrill."

"You mean prostitutes?"

"No, like party girls. Vegas show girls. The type who like parties thrown by rich guys out for a night of fun."

"What makes you think so?"

"Different perfumes, or lipstick on his clothes. Credit card bills."

"I need to see those, too. And his business records."

"Sure. He had duplicate computer disks and hard copies for his business deals because he got calls here at night."

"Point to his computer, and stand by with a bucket of water."

Chapter 3

Something worries me. Einstein thought his theory of special relativity was amiss because it suggested an expanding universe, not the then-accepted idea of a static one. Years later, Hubble trained a powerful telescope on faraway galaxies to learn that the universe is, indeed, expanding. We now know that it does so at an accelerating rate.

So Al wasn't wrong after all. That's a consideration as I wonder if I'm mistaken in my theories about this case, making the tedious work of reviewing Morrie's records useless. But I suppose, even though I'm not a genius, I'll forge ahead based on my best assumptions.

I've spent hours learning to operate Morrie's computer and searching through records. Having grown tired of the paper chase, I'm ready to pursue the other puzzle that needs to be solved, that being: how did Morrie's gun vanish from his hand and reappear in the killer's?

As does a cosmologist, I'm supposing a scenario by which this may have happened. Nope, I can't find that out by sifting through documents. So, this project is now on hold, and I'll drive downtown to see Bagley.

I arrive just before shift's end. Bill Wahr lets me in. Bagley frowns when he sees me, but pulls out a fat cigar and chews on it, trying to make the best of a bad situation, I suppose.

"Man," he says, "this is like *déjà vu* all over again."

"Yes, Yogi, Junior," I say. "Glad to see you, too."

He glances at the clock.

"I just need a minute, really." Yes, and Al showed us time is relative, too.

"Hmmph. What you got?"

"Just some hypotheses I'm running through my noodle."

"About the cosmos?"

"Everything's about the cosmos, Jeff, but I'm referring to Morrie's death."

"Max conquers the cosmos," he says, chuckling. Then he waggles a hand. "Maybe you shouldn't be working all that hard on this one, friend. I know you bill by the hour and all, but still . . ."

"Okay, I'll admit that I don't grasp the workings of the cosmos, but are you calling this a lost cause?"

"About as lost as they get," he says.

"I'm not ready to concede that."

His lips curl in a broad smile. "Well, I can't say that I blame you. The merry widow *is* pretty cute."

"She thinks I'm old."

"Hell, aren't we all?"

"I guess she's not. Relatively speaking, that is."

"Hey, I got a date with a cold beer. You have my total and unconditional surrender. What do you want?"

"A copy of the autopsy report, if you got it."

He rolls his eyes, then drops his foot to the floor and shuffles through some papers in his IN-basket. "I think it came in this afternoon. Yeah, here it is—the prelim. You want me to run one off for you? Unofficial, of course."

"That'd be a big help." Ah, the superb leverage of impending Miller Time.

"Anything else?" he says.

"That's it. Don't want to be a burden."

"Little late for that," he grumbles.

★ ★ ★ ★ ★

Swaying on my porch swing, I'm reading the report, my *Black's Medical Dictionary* resting beside me to be used as a reference for the few terms I must look up, which is about every third word. I'll discuss this with the coroner later, but I like to research things before taking anyone's valuable time. Seems I haven't yet found what I'm seeking.

The bullet wounds are thoroughly described, and disgusting, but that's life and death among the Homo Sapiens. We use our big brains, as Kurt Vonnegut terms them, to invent pistols so we can blow out each other's big brains. Not to mention nuclear devices, chemical weapons, and nerve gases. Rodney King, I hear your plea: "Why can't we all just get along?"

But until then, we've got to put away those who care more for their own agenda than the good of society. Which is all of us, let's face it, but at least most of us don't kill others to get our way. Stupid is as stupid does.

A hawk screeches as it wafts over the barn, scanning the pasture below. What a heady feeling it must be, soaring over everyone, seeing all that happens beneath you, being the lord of your realm. Just to have the ability to fly, much less the power of life and death over your minions.

But back to the report; I'm searching for causes of Morrie's other injuries. Here's a contusion on the right wrist, cause unknown. So if Morrie was right-handed, and his computer mouse suggests it, and he was holding the revolver in his right hand . . .

I see a definite scenario. Morrie stands there, gun in hand, talking to a guy he knows, not suspecting any danger, but maybe arguing over some beef they've got between them. The guy has other plans, and he's holding the pole behind his leg just in case he and Morrie don't agree.

So Morrie doesn't see eye-to-eye with what his visitor suggests. The man whips out the pole and whacks Morrie on the wrist. The pistol flies loose, and there's a scramble for it.

Was the other guy quicker and stronger? Morrie wasn't a big man. But when you're in a life and death situation, you become very powerful.

Still, Morrie's body shows no other scrapes, bruises, cuts, that is, nothing to suggest he's been in a scrap with another man over a pistol. That is, except for the circular bruise just below his sternum, cause also unknown. It's about 48 millimeters in diameter.

I'll bet I know what caused it.

Having studied the use of the police baton, I know that sticks, or clubs, or pool cleaning tubes can be used in various ways in fighting. Not only to strike with the side of the weapon, but also to poke with the end. Let's say that the guy knocks the gun out of Morrie's hand, then he pokes Morrie in the gut with the tip of the pole, pushing him back.

Next, the guy grabs the gun and blows Morrie away. Then he drops the pistol, tosses the pole into the greenery, and hightails it. Who's to say it wasn't a prowler?

The hawk sounds off again, soaring on the currents. Now he plummets like an arrow zinging toward the ground, striking into the waving grass. Then he rises, wings thrashing, clutching a wriggling mouse in his talons.

He sees all, knows all, makes all the decisions.

I have a theory about what may have happened to Morrie. If I tell the cops about it, they'll tell me not to do anything else, and to let them handle it from here. Then they might run out something, but they'll probably be too busy to do much, or it'll be too far-fetched for them to take seriously.

Or I could press forward, as daring and determined as a bird of prey. I could struggle to prove my client's innocence or at least implicate someone else in the crime. None of which a jury might even buy.

The hawk lands in the top of a tree to eat his kill. Some said man would never fly. But Wilbur and Orville just did it. Lindbergh flew across the Atlantic Ocean. Now astronauts soar into space.

I suppose I could flap my wings a little.

Another day, and our search for extraterrestrial intelligence goes on. Carl Sagan theorized that there could be a million planets in the Milky Way Galaxy with beings technologically advanced enough to try to contact other civilizations. But, naturally, there are problems involved.

We have to be on the same frequency in the signals we send and intercept. Plus, our Galaxy is a huge place to search, much less the rest of our universe. We must presume many things about how such signals might be sent from other civilizations, none of which may be true because of different physical laws which exist on those planets. We must know how to recognize a signal, then decipher it.

Also, other civilizations may have sent signals and then been destroyed. Or they might still exist, but they haven't yet reached a technologically advanced stage. Considering that Earth is 4.6 billion years old, and we've only sent transmissions at intervals during the past forty years, perhaps fifty-some, if you count radar and television signals, then it's clear there's a narrow window of opportunity.

Some scientists doubt many other planets have life forms with such a degree of intelligence. For instance, of the 50 billion species of animals on our planet, only one can hack it. That's us, pilgrim.

I've thought about these problems while clacking at Morrie's computer and assessing his records. Just as we don't know whether other civilizations would use electromagnetic transmissions in their attempts to contact others, I have no idea whether a lead to the killer is in this stuff. Just like our SETI projects, this is a shot in the dark.

Okay, hard feelings are engendered among people in business relationships. And that's not just postal workers spraying each other with automatic weapons. There are forms of theft, bribery, blackmail, and even threats and express violence in an effort to influence decisions or get revenge for real or imagined mistreatment.

Still, SETI projects have their limitations. The search for another intelligent culture is likened to finding a five-centimeter-long needle in a haystack thirty-five times the size of Earth. And if such a civilization is contacted, there's always the possibility that they'll immediately shoot a laser-type weapon that will evaporate our atmosphere. Or they'll just swoop in and eat us.

I hope my quest isn't that difficult or dangerous.

Vickie peeks in, as she's done a couple of times this afternoon, to see if I need anything. "Come in, Vickie, I was about to call you."

She sits down in an upholstered chair with a gooseneck floor lamp beside it. She's wearing a short white skirt which rides up as she crosses her legs. Her blouse is aquamarine, lending her eyes a cool tint. When she moves, her hair ripples like a golden brook.

I've been making piles of papers as though I'm accomplishing something. Patting a stack of letters, invoices, and checks relating to companies Morrie dealt with, I say, "Did you follow your husband's business?"

"In what way?"

"The nuts and bolts stuff. Did he discuss projects with you?"

"He talked about them some, but I found it pretty dull."

"Did you know his associates?"

"We didn't entertain them. They were contractors, architects, bankers. Morrie saw them at business functions." She gives a wry smile. "It seemed to me that they'd rather stuff themselves and suck down booze with pretty real estate agents or secretaries than drag their wives around."

"Would you recognize names of people he dealt with?" I shuffle through the papers. "Say Abraham Horowitz?"

"I've met Abe a couple of times. He's a prominent developer in Chicago. Morrie collaborated with him on a couple of projects there."

"So why did you move to Hillsboro?"

Her jaw tightens. "Morrie felt he saw an opportunity here. He imagined a suburban connection between Hillsboro and other towns closer to Kansas City. With his complex in place on the east side of town, he'd then buy up property along the interstate, hoping to eventually make a bundle."

"But you didn't approve of the venture?"

She shrugs. "There could've been some big gains, but I thought it was risky. He'd have had to start the impetus for growth and hope to lure other developers and contractors to join in. Rather like a gold rush."

"From what I know of the area, it seems a speculative venture."

"Morrie was a gambler. He liked big stakes, and big risks, too."

"But you aren't that way?"

"I grew up poor in Las Vegas, worked my way through college, then moved to Chicago. One night I met Morrie at a party. We hit it off and started dating. He always had plenty of money, and I suppose I'd grown used to the life. I didn't want to see him lose it all and us to wind up broke."

"Was he into that big a risk?"

She looks pensive. "I think it was chancy. Who knows how much it would have made or lost? He even had trouble getting his part financed."

"Who did finance the project?"

"He didn't mention details. He met with banks and other developers for months trying to get the project off the dime, but he had no luck. Then, all at once, he started working on final construction plans as though there was no problem."

"When was that?"

"Three, four months ago."

"The same time that you took out the life insurance policy?"

She gives me a hard look. "Morrie told me to do it. He was wrapped up in the details of getting the project in motion, so he asked me to take care of it, and he'd sign whatever was necessary."

"Why did he want you to take it out?"

"He knew it was a speculative project . . ." Her voice cracks, and her eyes mist up. "He said he didn't want me to worry about money if the deal fell through."

"But, Vickie, losing money in a business deal wasn't going to kill him."

"I know. He just seemed to equate this with his last hurrah as a developer."

"How was the project going?" I ask.

"At first he was energetic, almost euphoric. Then about two months ago he came to breakfast looking tired and sort of resigned. I'd say he may have been depressed."

"Did you talk with him about it?"

"Yes, but he just said he'd been working too hard and not sleeping well."

"Did you believe him?"

She purses her lips. "As I think back on it, he really wasn't acting like himself. He usually thrived on getting new projects off the ground. He loved challenges. It wasn't like him to let difficulties get him down."

I nod and riffle papers. "Who's Charlie Greeb? A contractor?"

"Yes, Morrie used him a few times. My impression was he was going to give Greeb a big part of the construction work."

"*Was* going to?"

"Until a couple of months ago, then he changed his mind and went with another contractor, Lugio Brothers Construction, based in Detroit."

I sift through contracts. "He did have some deals with them."

"They're probably okay. Morrie wouldn't pick anyone who wasn't. He liked things with his name on them done right."

Like his tombstone, I suppose.

Chapter 4

Morrie's records are full of corporate names. I jot down three construction firms, two real estate companies, and some others that I can't tell what they do. With each of them, Morrie had lots of correspondence, payments or receipts, or telephone contacts.

They're worth checking out, but I don't want this search to get too expansive. I learned from working in the FBI that the most critical point in an investigation is when you develop a good suspect, because then you can focus your efforts. Everything prior to that is simply shotgunning.

It's like SETI projects: we don't search the whole universe. In sending signals toward target planets, astronomers transmit from the same direction that light would be beamed to them from SN1987A, a supernova, assuming that they'd be studying it. So, I need to pick up the right signals from the proper areas.

There's also the prospect of jealous husbands or boyfriends. Despite what Vickie says, I think a skirt-chaser stays a skirt-chaser until impotence intervenes. But I can wait until tomorrow to ask her about that; no one needs to be upset right now.

As my Expedition rambles up my gravel drive, Binga bounds back and forth in front of the car, bellowing her cavernous bark. It seems to ward off burglars and salesmen. And it beats coming home to a silent house.

We cavort in the kitchen, anticipating the joys of a can of

dog food. Well, I'm leaning toward a burger. She gets some crunchies, topped off by chicken in gravy, which she bolts down in seconds. After waiting for this all day, just like that, it's over. Much like the hunger for sex.

A call to Amy Harrington gets me nowhere, as she's out. I leave no message, preferring to go by her office tomorrow. There are less pleasant things to do.

And I'll talk with the coroner. He may have insights into the killing that I haven't considered. Admittedly, there are more pleasant things to do.

I kick off my shoes, grab a brew, and flop in my chair. Thoughts of Vickie and Amy float through my head; it seems that women suddenly fascinate me. But, oddly enough, they don't seem to know I'm alive.

Maybe, like a dazzling supernova, I'll do something awesome one day, becoming famous and sought-after by hoards of women. Or maybe not. Binga comes up and lays her snout on my knee as if to say, "It's you and me, bub, together until the end." She's probably right.

The morning dawns bright and promising. Shorts and a sweatshirt seem appropriate, then I whistle for Binga to come join me on a walk. As we progress, she barges into the fields to chase bunnies and skunks, while I plod along on the gravel road.

Man is such a weakling. Not very fast, or strong, or able to fly, or burrow, or do anything which all the rest of the animal kingdom must do to survive. How could being a little smarter be such great protection against all those animals that are so physically superior?

Back home, I step into the shower. The cascading water feels great. Sometimes it's good to have sensitive skin instead of a tough hide like an alligator.

Morrie's papers sit piled on my desk; I stare at them, and they taunt me. I've got questions, so I call Vickie. She sounds groggy.

I apologize for the intrusion, then say, "I want to run some names past you—different companies and individuals—to see if you know them."

"Like who?"

"There's a Miller Construction in Kansas City."

"I think Morrie wanted them to take a third of the project."

"Who would have the other third?"

"An outfit in Vegas. I can't think of the name of it right—"

"Was it City Capital Investments?"

"I don't think so."

"How about Minnelli Promotions?"

"Yes, that's it. Like Liza, right?"

"I guess so. Did you ever meet—"

"Morrie saw them on trips to Vegas. I never went with him."

"What was Morrie's connection with The Mirage Hotel there?"

"He usually stayed there, is all. No business ties I know of. He was a high roller, especially fond of roulette, and they'd comp him a room when he traveled there."

I shuffle more papers. "Are you familiar with Carmine Lorenzo out of Los Angeles or a Jerry Parmontal in Miami?"

"I think they're both importers-exporters. Morrie would sometimes order supplies from overseas and get them cheaper."

I'll ask about Morrie's gal pals in person. I want to read

her face to make sure she's not holding out on me. "Will you be home today?"

"Try me after three."

"More tennis?"

"Beauty shop appointment. Nails, hair, the whole gamut."

So that's how the rich were living when I was hunting down criminals in seedy environs to protect them from the greed and violence of the poor. I can see how the lower half got envious and angry. Tried to grab a little for themselves.

Yes, they can also be uneducated, unmotivated, and unemployed. And they often use booze and/or drugs. But it's not my place to set mankind straight; I'd just like to catch this one killer.

"Make my day," Amy Harrington says, "and tell me you found the smoking gun that clears my client." She's leaned back in her chair wearing a dark blue suit with an ivory blouse with soft ruffles, looking fantastic.

"As you know," I offer, "the smoking gun is not a plus for us in this case. I'm trying to dig up some other people with motives to off Morrie."

"But you still have to establish means and opportunity."

"No one said my job was easy."

She smiles. "At least they haven't charged her yet. Guess they're waiting for the coroner's report."

I hand her the prelim. "Here's what they've got so far. I'm going to visit with the coroner in a little while."

"Is there a glimmer of hope for us there?"

"I hate to be cynical, but it doesn't look good."

"Did you drop by here to totally cheer me up?"

"No, Counselor, to cheer *me* up."

★ ★ ★ ★ ★

Gunther Wahrmach, the coroner, who is a qualified forensic pathologist, looks like a skinny vampire. Surely he's not. But he does have an interest in bloody death.

We're sitting in his office, which is in the same building as the police, giving me one-stop shopping. His degrees are displayed on the light green walls. There's a portrait shot of a woman and a pale teenage boy on his desk, which also holds stacks of papers and medical journals.

He hands me the autopsy photos, done in not-so-living color. They're vivid, clear, and disgusting. No one said murder was pretty.

Sifting through them, I ask, "Do you think either of these wounds could have caused his death?"

"Yah, Max," he nods his skeletal head, "Either the gunshot wound to the frontal lobe or the one to the left ventricle would cause incapacitation and/or instantaneous death."

"Couldn't do both shots to yourself?"

He tugs at the lapel of his wrinkled white lab coat. "Not at all. Besides, there was no stippling on either wound."

No gunshot powder imbedded in the flesh, I know. "Any other injuries?"

"What's that?" He pushes up silver-framed spectacles.

"Besides the gunshot wounds."

He flashes a crooked grin. "Aren't they enough? They seemed to do the job quite well."

"Oh, they did. But I was thinking of defensive wounds, or any bruises or scrapes that might suggest a preliminary attack."

"This was no knifing. There are no cuts on the hands or arms."

"But how about this?" I hand him the photo with the circular bruise over the solar plexus.

He studies it. "I saw that, but it didn't contribute to his death."

"Wouldn't it debilitate a person, maybe knock his wind out, if he were struck there with a hard object?"

He considers that. "I suppose it might," he says, nodding.

"How about this one?" The photo shows a bruise on the right wrist.

"Hmm. Gross contusion of the forearm. Could be a greenstick fracture of the radial bone."

"Which is?"

"A crack in his forearm."

"What might cause it?"

"Could happen from falling, but with the attendant contusion, I would guess he banged it on something or was struck."

I pull out a photo of the aluminum pole. "Could this do it?"

He looks at it a moment. "I'd say so."

"How about the circular bruise on the chest?"

He looks startled. "Do the measurements match up?"

"They seem to."

"Then you know more than you've let on."

"I'm just exploring a theory."

"I see." He shifts in his chair. "I can't tell any more about the contusion on the chest, but we still have the body, and I could X-ray the forearm."

"If you don't mind."

"I do have a client waiting, but he's not complaining yet."

Yuk. Yuk. "How long will it take?"

"Come back in an hour or so."

★ ★ ★ ★ ★

"So what are you tellin' me?" Bagley says, holding up the X-ray I glommed from the coroner.

"See that little line," I say, pointing with a ballpoint pen.

He angles it toward his desk lamp. "I guess so. It's not much."

"No, but it's a fracture. Morrie was struck hard on the forearm. My guess is with the pole from the pool scooper."

He scrunches his heavy brows. "So what?"

If I had the pole, I'd whack *him*. "It could signal foul play before he was shot. Say an intruder smacked him on the arm. Then poked him in the chest with the tip. Next he'd grab the dropped pistol."

"Are we back wasting time on the spectral prowler?"

"The footprint? Ciggie? Did you send them to the FBI lab?"

"Not yet. I'll get it done in a day or so."

"Do it. I'll call the lab, give them a heads up to process it."

"Okay, you've done your good deed for your client today. Now let me get back to work on a ball breaker case I caught."

I saw the paper. "The carjacking where the minister got popped?"

"Yeah, ain't that a bitch? People are up in arms."

"How come you caught that one, too?"

"Two guys got the flu, three on vacation, and two working a baby killing that's heating up. Plus the Captain is pissed 'cause I cleaned him out in poker."

"Haven't you learned to let him win some hands?"

"The guy's a lousy player. It's hard to even toss him some."

"So, you're not going to move on my client right away?"

48

"Can't tell you that. Draw your own conclusions, Sherlock."

"Don't forget to try for latents on the pole," I suggest helpfully.

"All done. Couple of partials, not good enough for comparison."

Damn. "Go back to work. But don't forget the intruder."

"Hey, the lady could have whacked Morrie with something."

"Why? She could just wait for him to put the gun back."

"Maybe she tried to make it look like someone else hit him, then aced him."

"So why throw the pole where the cops might not find it?"

"Max, you're giving me a headache. I'll look at that stuff as soon as I catch the dickhead that busted a cap on the priest."

"Thought he was a Methodist minister."

"Whatever."

"I suppose," I say, "we're all the same in the sight of God."

"Unless your client smoked her old man, then she'll fry in Hell."

"Don't get out the barbeque sauce yet."

Chapter 5

I call Vickie on my cell phone to tell her I'm coming to review more records. As I pull out of the lot, I see the Carlton Federal Building. Good memories there, mixed with dread, such as the day the guy tossed pipe bombs and shot up the place. Two people died that day. Now Morrie. Violent death seems such a waste.

When I turn onto Kansas Avenue, sun gleams on my windshield, and fresh air flows through the window. Life goes on. Yes, but at a cost.

The state capitol building rises to my right, a stately white limestone building topped with a copper-turned-green cupola, giving it a weathered, but majestic appearance. There's a huge Indian on top shooting an arrow toward the stars. Hope he's plenty strong.

As I near the Steak House, the cooking meat smells great, so I pull in for a sandwich. The good Lord sure knew what he was doing when he invented tangy barbeque sauce. It's finger-lickin' good.

Full as a tick, I drive past the White Lakes Mall, then turn west on 37th. Topping a rise, I view Vickie's house perched atop its hill. The hilltop looked better to me with the lush green look when it was covered with trees.

There's a note taped on her front door with my name on it. I open it to find a message: *If I don't answer the door, come on in. I'll be out by the pool.* It's signed *"V."*.

Ringing the bell brings no response, so I try the door, which is open. Seems she'd be scared of prowlers. But sometimes the rich think they're immune to the calamities of the world, even though it's just been proven otherwise.

I enter and call Vickie's name. Nothing. I walk to the back of the house. Through the closed patio door I see her sunning in a chaise lounge by the pool. Her electric green bikini is a dash and two dots.

She's reading a book and drinking what looks like a gin and tonic. The merry widow. But I probably shouldn't be so judgmental.

When I slide open the glass door, she looks up. There's a radio sitting on the patio table playing a plaintive Clint Black ballad. Wouldn't have picked her for a C&W buff, but there's not much choice in Middle America.

"Hi, Max. Come on out. Grab a beer if you want."

Oh, no. I'm here to review tons of more dry, boring records, not to enjoy the headiness of a glorious day. "Sure, I'll be right there."

One won't hurt. Might as well enjoy some fresh air after a morning spent with the caretakers of the dead and the dysfunctional. The coroner's office and the police station are not my favorite places.

I grab a Bud Lite Ice from the fridge. Twist off the cap and drop it in the trash. As I near the patio door, Clint finishes on a high note.

Easing outside, I slide the door closed. This is fantastic. The sky's blue, the water's sparkling, and the company's gorgeous.

Settling into a chair, I swig my beer. Chilled bubbles tickle my tongue. "Great day," I say.

"Yes, I like warm weather. In fact, when I move, I'll probably go to some beaches for a while, then settle back in Las Vegas."

"I'm still surprised Morrie wanted to come to Hillsboro."

She takes a gulp of the gin. "Morrie was hot on his money-making deal, you know. Besides, his partners thought . . ." She hesitates.

"Partners?"

"Oh, people he discussed potential deals with. Maybe more like business associates, or even advisors."

"Like who?"

She shifts in her chaise lounge, her tanned, taut flesh on the prowl. "They're in his files. I don't know many of their names."

I wait. Sometimes it helps to be still and silent. Like a cobra.

"Oh," she says, "like the Minnelli Brothers in Vegas."

"Minnelli Promotions? They're brothers?"

"Yes, Louie and Donnie. Also the Lugio Brothers in Chicago."

"Any more of these advisory types you know of?" I ask.

"No, that's all." She reclines on her chaise.

I'm recalling some more companies in the records. "How about Quality Construction in Salt Lake City?"

"I think that was a one-time project. He made some pretty good money on it, but he didn't like the people involved."

"And Sleek Enterprises? It's in Culver City, California."

She stiffens, then reaches for her drink. I wish she didn't have her damn sunglasses on, I'd like to read her eyes. She takes a sip, then says, "I haven't heard of that one. Morrie never did any projects out there, although he did take trips to L.A. to scout some out."

"When did he do that?"

"He went out there two or three times a year for the past

five years. Said it was fun to visit, but he wouldn't want to live there."

Now he has no choice. But maybe there's a cosmic connection among all the particles in the universe, and Morrie's spirit can zip around wherever he wants to go at any time. That'd be nice.

"Anyone else?"

She eyes me coolly. "I don't recall. You can check his records."

"I guess I'd better get to it." I drain my beer, gaze at the pool, then rise to climb aboard the treadmill of the middle class worker.

"Good hunting," she says as I depart.

Closing the patio door, I cut off Wynona warbling about losing a sweetheart. I've known the feeling. Country music echoes your pain.

Hours later, I remove my glasses, rub my dry eyes, and decide to call it quits for the day. I've made more stacks regarding companies and deals and expenditures and letters and phone calls. I'm still seeking the Holy Grail of a motive for anyone in this morass.

Vickie's comfy in the cushions of her living room couch reading *Vanity Fair*. She looks great in a pink and azure dress. Her hair's glossy, and in the lamp's light, her skin is sleek and glowing.

She glances up. "Find any clues, Sherlock?"

"Probably, but I can't identify them. It's like receiving radio signals from space, most of which don't mean more than static. You need a filter to find and decipher the ones that have a pattern."

"What are you talking about?" She's studying me as if I came from Mars. A theory says we're all descendants from there, so perhaps I did.

"I need to figure out where to concentrate my efforts. There's got to be some key that shows—"

There's a knock at the door. We stare at each other.

"I'm not expecting anyone," she says, touching her throat.

A loud voice outside the door says, "Police. Open up."

Looking out the peephole, I see two shapes, one I recognize. "It's Detective Bagley," I say.

She opens the door. "Yes, Detective, what can I do for you?"

"Can we come in?" he says. He's with a female detective with short, carrot-colored hair. I've seen her before, but don't know her.

"Of course," Vickie says, stepping aside. "What's it about?"

Bagley stares in her eyes. "You're under arrest, Mrs. Jacobsen, for Murder One. You have the right to remain silent . . ."

The redhead handcuffs Vickie and pats her down. I'm stunned. Why the sudden arrest? Why didn't Jack warn me? He's crashed into our placid world like a rogue asteroid devastating the planet.

After the shock of Vickie's arrest wears off, I go back to work at Morrie's desk. My investigation has become crucial. I've got to clear Vickie fast, or she'll be dodging dykes in the dungeon.

Two hours later, my cell phone twitters. "Austin Investigations."

It's Amy. "The judge set Vickie's bail at a half million."

"Can she come up with that much?"

"She's working on it, but she says it'll be hard."

"What about the insurance money?"

"The underwriter's dragging its feet, with its own investigators poking into it, trying to save itself the two mil. As my uncle in Texas says, 'They're tighter than a crab's ass.' "

"Words of wisdom from the second largest state," I say. "Is that where you get your accent?" She only has a trace, and it's charming.

"I lived in Texas until I was twelve, then my folks moved here. Most people don't notice anything but my flat Midwestern twang."

"I lived among native Texans for ten years," I say. "The armadillos, that is. I heard people trying to talk, too, so I recognize the sounds."

"Spare me the jabs, Max, I've heard them all."

"Sorry, I never met a sensitive Texan."

"You still haven't, I'm yanking your chain."

Story of my life. I'm at a loss for words, but she fills the void.

"So, anything hot on your end?"

"Just some theories that I have to check out."

"Better get on it, big guy, our client's not happy in the slam."

"If she didn't do it, I'll prove it."

"She just told me she didn't, and I think she's too scared to lie."

"But no one in jail will say, 'Yes, I did it. It was all my fault.' "

"Point taken, Mr. Lawman. So?"

"I'll keep you posted." I almost ask her to dinner, but it's a bad time. Maybe it'll pan out later, or maybe it's not meant to be. Few of the billions of asteroids zipping around in the asteroid belt collide. Maybe it's the same with people: the ones who need other people.

★ ★ ★ ★ ★

Still finding nothing helpful in Morrie's papers, I make a decision. Records are good for following a trail, but this case is about people. A lot of people. And I'm only one guy. I need help, now.

The main problem is, as in SETI projects, there's a lot of area to cover. There are connections between here and Chicago, Los Angeles, Miami, Kansas City, and Vegas. Not that I won't travel to those places, but I need help to winnow out the chaff from the wheat.

I could contact PIs in those cities. Some of them would do great work, some mediocre, some poor. And if the lousy one screws up the important lead, then none of the good work will be worth jack.

I review my murder binder, then pull out a pamphlet I stuck in there. It tells of a meeting of the Retired Agents Association. Lists the officers of the organization. I grab my cell phone and call a Don Reynolds in St. Louis.

"Max Austin," he repeats. "Are you the Austin in Kansas who broke the Oklahoma City bombing case?"

That's why his name seemed familiar. He was in Oklahoma City when the federal building got wasted in 1995, heading a key squad.

"Since the Ryder truck was rented in Junction City, I covered some leads, like everyone else in the Bureau."

"But if you hadn't gotten McVeigh's name at the Dreamland Motel, he would've been out on bond on the speeding and gun charges. He'd have been in the wind, probably for good."

"I'm glad things fell together. You guys did a great job there."

"Thanks." A pause. "Is there something I can do for you?"

56

I describe the case, then ask him to check for retired agents who are PIs.

"I'll find someone who can work our computer and call back."

Now things are cooking. And I recall something else: Phil Emerson, an agent I worked with in San Antonio, transferred to Vegas after a shootout in a hostage situation. He's retired, and he's had a couple of divorces, so I'll bet he's working security for a hotel there.

I also know agents who retired in L.A. and Chicago. And Miami. I think I'll head for the library to find phone numbers for old friends.

The computer here holds phone numbers and addresses for everyone in America. In the room, there's a scattering of high school kids with body piercings and tattoos, white-haired gents and ladies in casual clothes, and folks in suits or tailored dresses. I hit the keys.

My search works. I find numbers for all the agents except for the one in Vegas. He's keeping a low profile with an unlisted number.

I stride out into a cool, breezy evening, the sky dark, stars winking on. Cars roll past, their searchlights spearing the asphalt, tires thumping potholes. Much the way we try to steer through life.

As I roll down the street, I notice a sedan pull out of the library lot behind me. Funny, I saw no one leave the building after me. I slow, as though I'm not sure where I'm going. The other car slows, too.

It looks like a cop car. Not a black-and-white, but a Chevy, the kind detectives drive. I'm sure I've watched too many movies where the hero's in some crazy car chase with bad guys. My favorites were *Bullitt* and *The Rock*. But I don't have a hot car, there's no steep San Francisco hills, and those guys probably aren't even after me.

I'm passing Washburn University, and I turn into the campus. I slow as I approach the Petro Health Center. The other car turns, too.

I turn right, past the Kappa Sigma and Phi Delta Theta fraternities. Approaching a street, I signal a right turn. Instead, I drive into a parking lot beside the planetarium.

The car behind me slows, then makes the right turn. I take the driveway at the other end of the lot, then head back south past the health center and take the next exit back onto the street.

The Chevy's not in sight. I gun it for the intersection at 21st Street, just catching the left turn arrow, and squeal into the turn, headed east on 21st. Then I whip into a strip mall.

Stopping on the far side of a hardware store, I kill my lights. In a few seconds I spot a Chevy. But was it my tail? It looks like Bill Wahr in the passenger seat. But they're driving normally, not like cops who've just lost someone. This is very strange.

In a minute, I pull back into traffic. I seem to have ditched my tail, if there was one. Could be my imagination. After all, I'm not involved in anything that would call for anyone's scrutiny. Am I?

Chapter 6

When I roll into my driveway, Binga's standing guard, looking anxious. It's late; I'm sure she's starving. Inside, I fix her doggie bowl, saying, "All right, extra crunchies." Anything to get back in her good graces; no one likes dealing with a grouchy German shepherd.

I fry pork chops, stack the dishes, then grab the phone, drop into my chair, and call Miami. Marisol and I worked together in Puerto Rico years ago. She answers, and I say, "Is this Marisol Vegas?"

"Either you already knew that, or it's a very lucky guess."

"I've lost my salsa rhythm, *mi amor*. Can you help me find it?"

"Max! Good to hear your voice, *querido*, but I'm sorry, you never had any rhythm—I can't help you."

"*No importa*. When we danced, they just watched your moves."

"Bunch of *perros* in Puerto Rico, *tu sabes*. They're all horny. That's why I came back to the mainland."

"Don't kid me, you want to be the head of that chicken outfit." She's the Supervisor of Miami's Organized Crime Squad, a very impressive position at her young age.

"If Hillary can run for president, I can be the next Director. So, how's it going with you, big guy?"

"I don't play much beach volleyball, but I get around okay. In fact, I'm working a murder case here in the badlands of Kansas."

"You're pulling my hair."

"No, I do PI work. My client was charged with killing her husband, but I don't think she did it."

"Is there a connection in Miami?"

"Her husband was a real estate developer, had lots of contacts around the country. One was there—a Jerry Parmontal, owns the Bahama Mama Sales company. Heard of it?"

"Import-export business. Retail outlets. Like Pier 1, but funkier."

"Does Parmontal have any connection with your clientele?"

There's a stretch of silence. "I can't say what we're doing, but I recognize his name as a—how do you call it?—a fringe player. He's into shady deals, knows heavy hitters, does favors for low lifes such as himself."

"I know the type. Could I give you the dead guy's name?"

She agrees to check it out. "But will you promise to visit me soon?"

"You got it, Marisol. I'll even polish up my dancing."

"Start today. And practice, practice, practice."

I grab a Coors Lite, and Binga shadows me, whining for a biscuit. "Oh, all right," I say, and toss her one that bounces off her nose. Back in my chair, I call hotels in Vegas. Four major ones, with no luck. My fingers keep dialing.

"Caesar's Palace," answers a sultry voice that seems to say, "Step into my parlor and bring your wallet." I ask for Security, and a man answers. I say, "Is Phil Emerson on tonight?"

"Yeah, he's here, just a minute."

Jackpot. Who says you can't win in Vegas?

In a minute, the familiar voice says, "This is Emerson."

"I have a complaint. I was playing roulette and heard a leadfoot ex-fed in the ceiling above me. It rattled me, and I bet black by mistake."

"Don't tell me, is this Max Austin?"

"Phil! I thought so. You never could sneak around good."

"Jeez, I thought you were out to pasture. You in the hotel?"

"Nah, I'm in scenic Kansas. That was a joke."

"A lame one, as usual."

"Some things never change. So how do you like working security?"

"It's a job. Puts you in touch with a lot of hot babes."

"I thought you outgrew that, Phil."

"I suffered a third divorce, so I'm back on the prowl."

"You living on beans and bread?"

"You kiddin'? With the hotel's buffet, I gained ten pounds this past year."

"You were too skinny, anyway. Say, I've got a job that might interest you. Give me your home number, and I'll call you later."

"Sure. Make it tomorrow afternoon, it's my day off."

"Perfect. When's your shift end?"

"Different times. Four a.m. tomorrow. Nothing ever closes here."

"One of our essential American industries. Everyone with their noses to the grindstone."

"The better to sharpen the knives for the suckers."

"And on your rounds tonight," I say, "don't peek down too many dresses. I need your full attention tomorrow. It's important."

"Man, that's one of the biggest bennies of the job. But in your honor, I'll keep one eye closed when I'm tempted."

As I hang up, I find myself musing on dazzling lights, thousand dollar chips, and stunning women gliding across gaudy carpets. All that glitters is not celestial. But is the golden clue I'm seeking there at Caesar's, or only a Mirage?

Sitting in Morrie's leather swivel chair behind his walnut desk, I'm staring at the records that are all spread out. Vickie gave me a key to the place, and the cops are through snooping around, so I'm alone with the papers and the sounds a big house makes when there's a gusty fall wind, the leaves rattling. I still wonder why Morrie moved to this small burg.

He was nearly sixty, why take a gamble on a chancy project? Vickie said he liked risks, going to Vegas and all, but his business projects seem prudent. Couldn't he be a go-for-broke roulette player and a down-to-earth business-man?

Might be something to have Phil Emerson investigate in Vegas.

When I called Harry Billingsley in Chicago, he agreed to check Morrie's background. He was glad to do me a favor; besides, I put him on the payroll. I hope Vickie realizes it's necessary.

Once more I pull open desk drawers to study the items inside. A man's desk tells a lot about him. We keep secrets there, on purpose or just from careless habit. Anything from *Playboy* magazines to murder weapons.

But neither are there. In fact, I notice nothing unusual at all. Except . . .

In the back of the top right hand drawer, there's the corner of a dark document sticking up behind some enve-lopes. I didn't notice that before. But it's stuck in there good. So I open the drawer below, slide it all the way out, then get down on my knees and grope in the back.

A good tug, and it comes free. I straighten out the kinks. It's Morrie's passport.

Several trips are recorded and stamped within the past year. Two to Nicaragua, one to Switzerland, and one to the Cayman Islands. The latest trip, the second one to Nicaragua, was on June 29th, the date of my wedding anniversary. Another frozen memory in the vast tundra of time.

But why these expeditions? Business or pleasure? I wonder whether Vickie went with him on these trips; maybe the credit card bills can tell me.

The phone rings. Could be something urgent, so I answer.

"Who's this?" asks a man with a deep voice.

"Max Austin, a friend of the Jacobsen family. May I help you?"

"Where's Vickie?"

Abrupt sort. "She's indisposed right now."

"What's that mean?"

"She can't come to the phone, but I can give her a message."

A pause. "Tell her Louie called."

"What's it in regard to, Louie?"

"Umm, she'll know. Just tell her to call me."

Did I hear a "please" in there? Maybe he missed that day at kindergarten. "Does she have your number?"

More dead air time. "Okay, tell her 702-555-3344. Got that?"

"You bet. I'll give her the message."

From my previous calls, I recognize the area code for Nevada. When I call Phil Emerson, I'll ask him to get the subscriber to this number. I could call back under a pretext right now, but Louie might answer and recognize my voice.

He sounds like someone I don't want to get mad at me.

Checking the accordion file with the credit card bills, I pull out a sheaf of invoices and receipts for accounts: American Express, VISA platinum, and a titanium Master Card. There are some relevant bills.

The trips to the Caymans and Switzerland reflect round-trip airline tickets for one, meals at various restaurants, hotel bills, and not much else. Ditto for the trip to Nicaragua in November of last year. But the Nicaragua trip this June was different. There are charges for two airline tickets. Costs for meals are higher, and also the hotel rooms.

Either Morrie had a girl accompanying him on the later trip, or Vickie went along for the ride. So why didn't she go with him to the Caymans and Switzerland? They seem like places a wife would enjoy visiting.

But Nicaragua? Not that it's not nice there. Many Americans are settling there, now that Costa Rica is becoming too expensive.

I'll ask Vickie about that. Should I question her about Louie, too? No, I'll wait to see what Phil finds out on the number.

Which reminds me that I need to contact some people myself. I'll start with the construction company in Kansas City that turned Morrie down on his project. It'll take me an hour to drive there.

"Do you have an appointment?" asks the plumpish receptionist with smooth caramel skin and large mahogany eyes.

"No, but tell Mr. Miller it's about Morrie Jacobsen. And it's urgent."

She looks dubious, but she rings him, then hangs up and smiles. "He says to go right in." She points. "Down the hall, first office on the right."

As with random cosmic rays, the chaos theory, and dumb luck, sometimes things go right.

I knock on the door. A booming voice says, "Come on in, Partner."

I do, and Mr. Miller stands up behind his desk, all six-foot-seven, with lots of muscle. He's forty or so, but balding. I introduce myself.

He grips my hand with a paw the size of a catcher's mitt. The bookshelves are filled with basketballs, trophies, and team pictures. There's a photo of him with former Jayhawk coach Larry Brown.

Back then I worked in New York, then Chicago. Didn't follow KU or KSU, either one. I don't much now, except to be able to converse with avid sports fans, which is almost everyone in the Midwest.

He settles back in his giant chair. "You're here about Morrie?"

"Yes, I'm working with his widow's attorney."

"I was sorry to hear about his death. Any idea who did it?"

"His wife saw and heard a prowler, but he hasn't been found."

He shakes his head. "I guess these days you never know, huh? Of course, around here someone's always getting popped, but you'd think it'd be safer there in a small town than here in the big bad city."

"You'd think."

"I liked Morrie. We went to dinner and around. He was okay."

"That's good," I say. "Where did you go besides dinner?"

"Huh?"

"You said 'to dinner and around.' What did that include?"

He shifts in his chair. His arms look thick and strong. "When customers or associates are in town, I sometimes take them on the fun circuit."

"What's that?"

"Your strip clubs and topless bars, shit like that. Morrie seemed to like 'em. He'd sorta let his hair down and all. Although . . ."

I wait, but he's fiddling with a pen. "Although what?"

He frowns. "I didn't mean to get into personal stuff. Morrie was a good guy. I'm sorry he got killed."

"Maybe personal stuff is important."

He stares at the bookcases. "Hmm, maybe. He was just . . . I mean, he'd get to drinking pretty heavy, and he'd get a little wild."

I nod. And wait. Looking at him.

"Oh, he'd want lap dances, maybe try to squeeze some titties. Couple of times . . . but I don't see it makes any difference now. Poor guy's dead."

"Each piece of the puzzle helps. I need to track down his killer."

"Well, a couple of times Morrie wanted to visit a cathouse."

"Did you take him?"

"Sure, I'm not going to turn down a contact like Morrie."

"But you turned him down on building the industrial park."

"Yeah, but he might have other ideas in the future. Or we might want him to join us on a deal. He was a good connection."

"Why did you turn down his project?"

He taps the pen against his lips, then lays it on the desk.

"It seemed like too big a complex for that area. Too much commitment was called for. Basically, I didn't think it'd turn a profit."

"Why not?"

He reaches in a drawer and comes out with a map. "Look," he says, spreading it on the desk, "Kansas City has sprawled out in these directions."

"Right."

"There's lots of expansion between Kansas City and nearby towns, like Lawrence. But when you get as far away as Hillsboro, there's no connection. Why sink so much money into a project?"

I think it over. "Why *did* Morrie have his mind set on it?"

He leans back in his chair and regards me over tented fingers. "I wondered, too. Even discussed projections with him, but he wouldn't listen."

"Did he give you an explanation?"

"He said he had to finish it, and there was no turning back."

I wonder what the heck Morrie meant by that?

Chapter 7

I stroll around my yard, caught up in the pleasures of autumn. The air against my face feels cool and crisp and clean. Hedgerow trees glow a vibrant yellow and black oaks a burnt sienna, while the silver maples flash leaves of glossy pewter. Shining sumacs have gone the color of the fresh blood I recently viewed and can't forget.

I toss a tennis ball for Binga. The sun settles behind the hills, and the horizon goes blue and purple, streaked with orange. Stars and planets should be visible soon. Wish I could view them tonight, but like scientists who discover more planets in our galaxy, I sense that I may find more suspects in Morrie's special universe.

Sometimes I question whether I should be working this case. Maybe I should let the police handle it. But they have other jobs, and this could be far-reaching because of Morrie's many relationships.

Also, the police tend to do better with local players. The cast of characters in this crime may get too large and far-flung. I'm afraid the cops will fall back on their number one suspect, Vickie, as the most practical solution to a messy crime.

There's no solid reason to think someone besides Vickie may have caused Morrie's untimely departure from our sphere, but just as we're sure that billions of neutrinos bombard the Earth daily, I think there's more to this crime than meets the eye. Morrie was pushing a project, having problems finding financing or partners. Miller in Kansas City turned him down, thinking the project too speculative.

Also, Morrie had a deal with Charlie Greeb, but dropped him. Then the Lugio Brothers in Detroit joined in, and Morrie got funding from Minnelli's Promotions in Vegas. Morrie mentioned to Mr. Miller that he couldn't back out of the deal.

Just like the rocks zipping around in the asteroid belt, it seems as if there was lots of movement in Morrie's business plans.

Another interesting factor is the way Morrie tended to flaunt the law. He'd get wild, as shown by his arrest record in Kansas City: drunk in public, plus assault and battery when he punched a bouncer at a topless joint. There was also a charge for battery of a woman he claimed tried to rob him, but I suspect was probably a pro who got short-changed.

Add in Morrie's business contacts in Chicago, Las Vegas, Kansas City, Miami, and Los Angeles, together with the curious trips to Nicaragua, Switzerland, and the Caymans, and I see a crazy quilt pattern that Morrie may have been tangled in. But I still don't know the motive for his murder. Maybe a prowler really did, like a chance comet, swoop out of the sky to smack him.

But it doesn't fit my sense of order. Comets are un-predictable. Fortunately, murder seldom is.

I don't have much expertise in homicide cases, but I've found that the same basics apply in any type of investiga-tion. Someone did the crime for love, money, or revenge. There are many variations on those themes, but they boil down to the same fundamentals.

Binga's been waiting patiently, panting, her tongue hanging down, so I fling the ball a last time like a rocket bound for Mars, and the old gal lumbers after it in slow motion. We all lose a step or two, eventually. It's inevitable, but sad to see.

I settle into the porch swing, thinking that because I'm the most motivated to learn that someone other than Vickie pulled the trigger on Morrie, I'd better stick with trying to find the guy. If John Glenn can go back into space at his age, I would think I could solve another mystery a couple of years after retirement.

Lying on the swing beside me, the phone rings, and I pick it up.

"That you, Max?" It's Harry Billingsley in Chicago.

"Hey, Harry, are you snowed in for the winter?"

"Man, it's fall. The temp's only been below zero twice so far."

"That's balmy by your standards."

"Short sleeve weather. Wish the Cubbies were still playing."

He's a big fan. Go figure.

"Be happy, Harry. If they're not playing, they're not losing. Anyway, what's shakin' there, man?"

"I ran that criminal check on your victim and his spouse. She seems clean, aside from a couple of speeding tickets, but old Morrie's got a past."

"How so?"

"He's got two DUI's, plus he got in a fight outside a bar one night and whacked some guy on the head with a tire iron."

"Did he hurt him bad?"

"Glancing blow, caused a cut on the scalp. I figure they were too drunk to hurt each other. He got tossed in the tank for the night."

"Guy sure couldn't hold his booze. Was there any indication of spousal abuse?"

"Funny you should bring that up. Two calls of marital disturbances, but when the cops got there, no one pressed charges."

"Not surprising. Anything on Abraham Horowitz?"

"Nothing you could hang your hat on. He's been a developer here for years. Always tight with City Hall. I talked to a couple of active agents, and they say he's considered close to the Mob, plays golf with higher ups and all, but they've never caught him dirty."

"My kind of town. Any indication Morrie had ties with them?"

"Haven't found anything, but if you want, I'll dig some more."

I consider it. Chicago, Kansas City, Vegas, all involved. The FBI handled a case a decade ago where the mobsters in those cities skimmed the take at Vegas casinos. Maybe there's a connection here. "Could you stay on it? It could help."

"You bet. I've had fun playing the old games."

Hanging up, I decide to try Los Angeles again. If there's something going on nationwide, I'm sure they're involved. Sammy Tiburon picks up on the second ring. I fill him in on what I'm working.

"Max, you always did get involved in intricate bullshit." We worked together in Brownsville, Texas. Some of my white-collar cases took months to work and prosecute. Sammy preferred to catch dopers with the goods in hand.

"There may be zip to all this," I say. "Could be nothing more than a jealous wife aced her cheating hubby. But he has a jaded past and a lot of strange business connections." I run it by him.

"I haven't heard of Carmine Lorenzo. What was his company?"

"Sleek Enterprises," I say. "Address in Culver City."

"Sounds oddball, but then a lot of things do in L.A."

"You've been out there so long I'm surprised you still notice."

"I hear that, *cunado*. I'm living in the Hollywood Hills with a pool, even driving a vintage Porsche."

"You *have* gone native."

"Don't knock it. I've been doing security work for Columbia Studios, and, man, I run across more fine women. It's fantastic."

"I don't know that I can match your princely salary at the movie lot, but I can get you two hundred dollars a day, plus expenses."

"That's fine, I don't get squat for pay here. The trick is to meet someone and become a technical adviser for a movie or TV series. That's when you rake in some serious coin."

"Sounds like paradise. Titans of the silver screen all around."

"Don't kid yourself. Most of 'em are egotistical assholes."

"You're bursting my bubble. So go catch a bad guy for me."

"That's what I'm here for. I'll call if I get anything."

"Don't phone to tell me about the starlets."

"But that's some of my best work."

The perennial girl-chaser. But Sammy's a top-notch sleuth. I'm hoping he may turn over the right rock on the beach.

Morning dawns fresh and bright, giving me hope that today I'll get it right, not saying things I shouldn't, messing up simple projects, and scarfing down fattening foods. There's a quality of life in the country that eases the anxiety that only humans seem to feel. Nature makes it clear that the problems besetting people in their rushed world of cars, calculators, and computers are simply so much bullshit.

Binga stretches, then trudges out the door for her ritual of barking, sniffing, and peeing. I sit in my porch swing with a glass of milk and watch the birds in their struggle at the stocked feeder. They approach the level of bickering, blustering, and ballyhooing of the humans on Wall Street and other playpens for the human comedy.

Of course, animals have their own games. Twice I've seen rabbits playing "Hop the Bunny," an intriguing contest. When I was a kid, the bunnies spotted me right away and scurried into the brush, so I thought my eyes had tricked me. But I observed the sport again two years ago, and the bunnies were caught up in the action, so they didn't notice me.

The players face each other, their noses twitching. One charges at the other, hard and fast. The targeted bunny waits until just before the collision, then leaps into the air. The attacking one passes beneath, then stops, whirls about, and the contest continues. I suppose all living things need a diversion from the daily grind.

But this morning I can't study nature's lessons. I need to concentrate on the games people play, including murder most foul. There are a lot of tentacles to this mystery creature I'm wrestling, and they may be far-reaching.

I like to do the legwork on my own investigations. Being honest, I enjoy the challenge between myself and the criminal who did the evil deed. I hope to have the wits to solve the puzzle and be able to identify him.

But in this case I'll have to rely somewhat on others, coordinating their moves and encouraging their dedication. Not that I don't trust the other agents and Detective Bagley, but I'd rather screw something up myself, then take the blame. So I'll do as much of the investigation myself as I possibly can.

I'm bothered that Morrie contacted Abraham Horowitz, Mr. Miller, and Charlie Greeb about his project, then hooked up with totally new companies: Minnelli Promotions in Vegas and the Lugio Brothers in Detroit.

I might talk to Horowitz in Chicago, but first I think I'll contact Charlie Greeb, a contractor Morrie worked with several times, then dumped. He probably knew Morrie well and might be bitter enough to dish a little dirt about the companies Morrie contracted with on the project. Besides, Greeb is headquartered in Kansas City.

I phone Greeb's company, talk with the receptionist, then reach Greeb's personal secretary. "So you're with the police, Mr. Austin?"

"Not exactly. I'm a private investigator, but I'm working with an attorney, as well as the Hillsboro police, on a murder investigation."

"I'm sure Mr. Greeb will help you if he can. He's in a meeting at the bank now, but his schedule's open this afternoon."

"That's great."

I'll take a walk and pump a little iron. Then I'll drive back to Vickie's. People often leave information in places they don't expect to be checked, and by giving me the key, Vickie implied I could snoop.

Besides, she's my client. The more I know about why Morrie was killed, the better off she'll be. At least, for her sake, I hope so.

As I survey Vickie's huge house from the steep driveway, I sense it's taking on the pallor of death. Maybe it's because no one is around at the moment, or maybe it's because evil lurks, waiting to get someone else.

Which I guess would make me the prime candidate for mayhem. Sometimes I wish I'd never seen *Psycho*. Going up a flight of stairs alone in an empty house can sure play havoc with taut nerves.

But it's my job, man. So I ease out of the Expedition and approach the looming house, key in hand. There are no sounds coming from inside. As I enter, I smell staleness setting in. I'll open a few windows, maybe the patio door.

Crossing to the sunroom, I slide open the glass door, and peer out at the pool, the sun glaring off its placid surface. Birds chirp, twitter, and flap in the trees, and somewhere far off, a dog barks. Why would someone invade this piece of paradise to murder Morrie?

Or, as my client insists, it could have been a burglar who got surprised by Morrie charging out there with gun in hand, and who, with his adrenaline pumping and heart thrashing, managed to grab the weapon away from Morrie and plug him. Then Vickie picked up the gun and shot at the guy as he was crashing through the bushes.

She says she's a good shot, why didn't she hit him? But if she fired at a shadow and a sound instead of a clear target, there'd have been little chance of doing so. Besides, it's very hard to hit a moving target.

Still, that reminds me, the third bullet fired from Morrie's gun was never found. The uniforms looked for it a while, and Detective Bagley and I checked around some more, but no luck. Maybe I'll try another search.

Out through the side gate, I skirt the bushes around the pool to the other side where I found the thread caught on the fence. There are bushes and slender maple trees, any of which could have deflected the shot. But the bigger elms, oaks, and cedar trees would have stopped the bullet easily.

In fact, there are two trees in what was probably the line of fire, considering where Morrie's body sprawled and where the burglar went over the fence. So, figuring the shot was aimed at the guy's back, I study the bark on the trees, looking for a small, circular hole.

I soon realize this is like looking for a flea on an elephant's back. The tree I'm beside is a hearty pin oak, its branches reaching skyward. Its arms will stay outstretched for a lot longer than mine, unless researchers produce a total gene and body replacement.

Now I spot a woolly caterpillar inching upward, at about the height of a basketball goal. Heavy black-and-orange coat; some people say that signals a cold winter. The critter pauses, seeming to be trying to squeeze its way into an opening in the tree's rough bark.

It can't fit, so it continues its slow movement up the trunk, probably trying . . . wait a minute, don't tell me. I pace back around the fence, let myself into the garage, and come out carrying a ladder. Back to the tree, then up I go to inspect the hole the caterpillar couldn't penetrate.

It's small, round, and shallow. Something's stuck in it. With my knife, I dig and pry, finally slipping the point in under the flattened metal slug, working it out of the wood, and popping it into my hand.

Big enough to be a .357 Magnum bullet. If ballistics can be done on it, it could prove to be a round fired from Morrie's gun, which would substantiate Vickie's story. Except for one thing.

Why is the bullet lodged in the tree trunk ten feet above the ground? She wouldn't have hit anyone that way. Was she just excited, firing wildly, or was there some plan to the scenario?

I juggle the slug in my palm, trying to make sense of the

matter. Maybe this shot was fired some other time. But Vickie said she always shot at a firearms range. Besides, there are the neighbors.

As I close the patio door, I'm thinking I'd better call Bagley.

But standing there, I get a funny feeling. Something's not right. I listen, hearing no unusual sounds, then I realize that's the problem.

I open the patio door and hear the squawks of blue jays, which I imagine I was hearing when I came in the door. But, as in *Ace Ventura: Pet Detective*, when the door is closed, it blocks sounds.

Could this be the mistake I was concerned about? Could both Einstein and I have goofed? Or were we right all along?

Chapter 8

Could Morrie have heard a noise coming from the shed at the far end of the pool? Not with the patio door closed. So if Vickie was lying about that, she was probably lying about the rest. Also, could she have heard Morrie talking to another man? No way.

So was the door open that night? It was warm, maybe they had it cracked for fresh air. But when Morrie went outside to check on the noise, he probably would have closed the door, just to protect Vickie.

Or maybe he slipped out, trying to be quiet. Didn't close it so as not to make any noise. Hoped to sneak up on whoever was out there.

I need to ask Vickie about that without tipping her off about what I'm after. But she's pretty astute. And I may be getting rusty.

As I search through the files, preparing for my interview with Charlie Greeb, it reminds me of the first time I set up my telescope and pointed it toward Arcturus. Seemed it'd be simple to pinpoint the bright star, but there was a lot of other stuff up there gleaming at me. Just as then, I'm not sure if I'll know when I find what I'm seeking, no matter how obvious.

There are the usual contracts, work invoices, letters, and duplicate checks for work performed. No indication of any problems between Morrie and Greeb; no nasty letters or lawsuits. They seem like two business pros.

So why couldn't they get together on this deal?

My cell phone warbles. A secretary says Greeb will be in his office the rest of the afternoon. I say I'll be there in an hour.

Rolling along I-70, I recall what Mr. Miller said about Morrie's project being too speculative, considering its location. It *is* empty out here, with pastures to either side of the interstate. But Morrie was a veteran developer; why didn't he see the problem?

He told Mr. Miller that he had no choice about doing the project. That strikes me as an odd remark. But maybe he only meant that he was too committed to the development by then to back out.

Or maybe his "advisors" insisted on their wishes. I'll dissect his dealings with Minnelli Promotions and the Lugio Brothers. And I'll check Vickie's background, too. What with the large life insurance policy and the stray bullet, I sense traces of something in the air.

And just as finding the cosmic microwave background gave us proof of the Big Bang Theory, I think the static on my investigative receiver might signal a design to this system of chaotic parts.

On the outskirts of Kansas City, the rail yards are clotted with boxcars spread chock-a-block like a child's toys. Once a thriving part of the economy, the area looks barren and depressed. Greeb's office is in a dun-colored building near the yards. Cement mixers sit in a sandy lot to one side, with a dozen dusty cars parked in front. Two big yellow cranes loom in back like dinosaurs peeking over a boulder.

After a short wait, the receptionist, a pretty Asian girl, tells me I can go in. I follow a gleaming linoleum trail to an open office door. Greeb's sitting at a large oak desk with a phone cocked to his ear.

He's late forties, as skinny as Ally McBeal, and wearing a

shirt as white as a priest's collar. Motioning me in, he then points at a chair in front of his desk. "Okay, that works for me. I'll call you later."

After he hangs up the phone, we both stand up and shake hands. I flash my license, and he glances at it and nods. "You're looking into Morrie Jacobsen's murder?" he says. "I hear his wife's in jail."

"For the moment."

"So you don't think she did it?"

"May I ask, do you?"

He cocks his leg up on his desk and grasps his knee with both hands. "I never met her, and Morrie didn't talk about her. I don't have an opinion on that situation."

"I'm also interested in your connection with his project." I open a folder. "You had some big construction contracts with him."

He nods. "But then he went with the Lugio Brothers."

"That's what puzzles me. What happened?"

He sighs, picks up a pack of cigarettes, and offers me one. I decline. He lights up, saying, "Terrible habit. I quit every month." He takes a deep drag of his Lucky. I'm watching who smokes what.

"All right, we did have a deal," he says. "Morrie shocked me when he came back a month later and said he had to renege."

"You didn't challenge him? Didn't try to enact default clauses?"

He lays the weed atop a Pepsi can on his desk, then leans forward on his arms. "Morrie and I always got along, and he'd never backed out before, so I figured he had a good reason. I just let it go."

"You lost a pretty juicy contract."

He shrugs. "There's always other projects."

"Did he tell you why he was going with them?"

He mulls it over. "Something to do with the financing package."

"From Minnelli Promotions?"

"I don't know. I don't think he said."

"Do you know anything about the Lugio Brothers?"

"Just heard of them. They don't do much in this area."

"How about a Sleek Enterprises in Culver City, California, or Bahama Mama Sales in Miami? Ever deal with either of them?"

"Never heard of 'em."

"One more thing. Did you think Morrie's project was sound?"

He puffs out a stream of smoke. Then he has a sudden fit of coughing. In a minute, he says, "You ask good questions."

"I've had a lot of practice. I'm a professional snoop."

"It's pretty common for businessmen to go out on a limb sometimes. Look at Ford's Edsel and Coca-Cola dropping the original. I think Morrie would've taken a bath on that project." He coughs some more. "I've got to give these things up."

I wonder whether Morrie's killer has a smoker's hack.

Back on the highway, my mind spinning, thoughts whirling freeform, colliding, accreting, much as the Earth formed from bits of dust, I'm getting no pattern from which a global theory will emerge. I'm going to study the blueprints, but on first glance Morrie's project seemed grandiose. And there's the old realtors' mantra: location, location, location.

Prairie grasses are going russet, horses grazing, hay stored. Pretty country, and the interstate affords quick access to Kansas City, but by the time you get to where Morrie's industrial park would be, you're pretty far from the beaten path. Maybe thirty or forty years from now, with population growth, it would work.

Why were his "partners" so insistent on the project? Who, exactly, are we talking about? Do they have any connection with Morrie's death?

Better contact the other agents. I need some vital clue to ignite my investigation. Maybe even a bolt of electricity, such as hit Frankenstein, making him rise up and stumble off to his strange destiny.

Traffic slows as we approach some highway construction work. A blond girl wearing an orange vest, who's poured into jean cutoffs, holds a sign that says SLOW, presumably for workmen watching a machine roll over a stretch of hot asphalt. Saddle tan, she flashes a smile at each car. Beats the sight of a filthy guy with a beer belly.

And it reminds me of Morrie's peccadillo about chasing women. What was wrong with him? A plethora of testosterone, I suppose.

Could this case involve the hoary theme of sex rearing its ugly head? As in: all murders are committed for love, sex, or money. Or as in Randolph Scott or Charles Bronson movies, there's also the smoldering desire for revenge.

Still, imagine Morrie, at his age, getting arrested for DUI, assault, and domestic disturbances. Booze and women seem to be what were at the heart of his problems. Or rather, his inability to deal effectively with either.

Maybe that character defect led to his death. Ah, I'm past the construction, traffic surges ahead, and now, feeling the rush of cool air pouring through the window, I sense I'm cruising in the right orbit.

Back home, I stroll around the yard with Binga, throwing a new yellow tennis ball for her to chase. "Go, speed demon," I shout, and she seems to charge a bit harder. We can all use encouragement sometimes.

She's lost the ball and searches this way and that. I survey the countryside, a serene view of rolling hills splashed with yellows, reds, and oranges. If only Sharon were here to take walks with me and watch romping squirrels. Kiss and hug. Nothing fancy; we both liked the simple life, but it's better to have someone to share it with.

Binga's back, panting but proud, and I wait a few seconds, then heave the ball hard one last time. She gets sore in the hips after running, but I think the fun outweighs the pain. At least, as in all of our lives, I hope it does.

As I turn toward the house, I imagine Sharon swaying on the porch swing. Then I think of Amy Harrington. Would she be happy sitting there? Would she like the natural world out here? Am I delusional?

Back inside, I feed Binga, then snag a couple of pretzels and a Diet Coke. I grab the phone and dial Miami. Lucky me, I get Marisol.

"Max, I was going to call you when the catastrophes abated."

"I can call back later."

"Man, you've been there. Things never settle down. Always the dull roar of disaster about to overwhelm us like a giant wave."

"I hear that. Sorry to bug you, I just wondered if you'd found anything. I'm trying to put together some jerry-rigged theories."

"Hold on . . . here it is. *Este,* Jerry Parmontal does run the Bahama Mama Company, but he's got some other side-lines."

"Such as?"

"Numbers, sports action, fronting groups that import

cocaine from Colombia. We've got a sting operation that I never mentioned, and he's heavy into smarmy stuff, including kiddy porn."

"What a prince."

"We think he merchandises stuff between China and here. The old Oriental swap meet. Show us yours, we'll show you ours."

"International smut. Warms the cockles. Take him down."

"That'll happen soon. Damn, here comes my snoopy secretary. I'll call you if I come up with anything more. Good luck, *amigo*."

"And good luck to you, *mi amor*," I say to a humming dial tone.

Downing a couple of brain benders helps me endure watching the national news. Sometimes it's a mystery why our whole nation isn't depressed. Meanwhile, a potpie steams in the oven, and Binga gnaws a rawhide bone, often drowning out the announcer as her incisors screech down the edge.

When the news ends, I punch the remote, killing the screen. Ah, silence. Except for the chomping over there.

I pick up the folder with Charlie Greeb's information, leaf through it, and wait for a starburst of insight to shoot across my brain. I'd settle for a solar flare knocking my neurons haywire for a minute if I could put together a cogent thought when I recovered. Maybe another cold silver bullet would help.

Returning to my chair, I pause beside my telescope, pull out a handkerchief, and dust it off. What a pity. I love studying the stars, constellations, and galaxies, and I haven't had time to—

Hmm. Galaxies, such as the Milky Way, are often formed as spirals. Our galaxy is a barred spiral—a thicker cluster of stars in the middle—which in a side view looks like a pregnant Frisbee.

Spirals have arms that extend from the center of the galaxy. The whole system whirls as one, with gravity holding it together, even though everything in our universe keeps expanding outward due to the Big Bang. There's a force that controls all parts of the galaxy.

Say Morrie operated as a lone star, then suddenly he got caught up in the force. He gets sucked in as part of the system. He changes business partners, his means of operation, maybe his project.

Just as Chandra, our X-ray telescope in outer space, can give us far more insight into the workings of the universe, I need—

Just what I didn't need. My cell phone to ring. I give my standard business greeting.

"You sound so official it makes me laugh."

"Phil, is that you?"

"Don't you hear the click of chips in the background?"

"And blue-haired ladies plunking their Social Security bucks into the slots?"

"There you go with your mushy social conscience."

"Sorry, man. What's up?"

"Couple of things. Seems Morrie was a fair-sized gambler, nothing gaga by Vegas standards, but enough to get comped. Usually at The Mirage. And that's where your mystery phone is."

"In the call from my buddy, Louie?"

"Right. It wasn't the main number, but it went to an office there. I know a guy who works security there, and he says it's for Louie Minnelli, who's sort of a suave enforcer, keeping the dealers and the sharpies in check."

"The better for the mobsters to skim profits themselves."

"Things never change, you know, they're just slicker at pulling it off."

"Did you do a background check on Minnelli?"

"Yeah, he's had some busts, usually getting too rough with people. He's a hothead. But he skated on most of them."

"*Most?*"

"You're still a good listener, Max. Four months ago he got involved with a local hooker. He smacked her hard a couple of times. In fact, she had a weak heart, and she died in the hospital."

"Did he get convicted?"

"Never went to trial. It was a confusing mess, with two witnesses saying the girl threatened Louie with a knife, and he was defending himself. The DA offered unintentional manslaughter, and he pled, got one year, suspended."

"Sounds like life is cheap there. Were the witnesses reliable?"

"One was another hooker."

"And the other?"

"I thought you'd never ask. It was your stiff: Morrie Jacobsen."

"Where'd this happen?"

"In one of the rooms at The Mirage."

"I'm surprised they didn't get the whole mess sanitized," I say.

"They probably would've, but there was an off-duty cop in the room next to them who went to see about the commotion."

"Send me the full report. And I may take a run out to see you."

"Let me know when you're coming, pal, and I'll get you a good suite."

But as I hang up I realize that when I go, I'll be staying at The Mirage.

Chapter 9

During the night lightning crackled like sparks from a grinder. The house shuddered, buffeted by a gusty north wind, and rain cascaded on the roof as if from a giant bucket. This morning the sky remains as gloomy as the outlook for this case, and a cheerless drizzle drifts over my pasture.

Wipers slapping, I head into town to chat with Vickie at the jail. Amy told me Vickie's unhappy with her accommodations. Maybe she'll be primed to give me some hints suggesting who did the deed to Morrie.

I wheel into the visitors' lot at the county jail. Inside, the air is stuffy, almost as confining as the walls and bars. It's depressing to see the human spirit held captive, bound by rock and steel and despair.

A guard escorts me to a sterile box they call an interview room, one of three in a row: A, B, and C. We're at C, which, just as the others, has a metal table set in the center, bolted to the floor. Two folding chairs. I sit down in one, slouching for comfort, and lay my notebook on top of the table.

There's some grit, like tiny specks of sand, and I brush it off on the floor, imagining God flinging the initial bits of dust into the void, which coalesced, then exploded, forming our universe. This gets me to contemplating the meaning of life. All at once, I see the pattern, it's suddenly clear that—

A bulky guard with slicked-back hair, who smells like the lotion used in barber shops when I was young, opens the door, wheezes, "Here you go," and points for Vickie to sit down in the other chair.

I greet her and thank the guard. He grunts, slams the steel door, and locks it. I've often sat in rooms like these without a weapon, across from some buffed-up con who's serving a ton of time and doesn't give a damn about anything; it's not a good feeling.

"Where'd you get the black eye?" I ask.

"I had a difference of opinion with another inmate, but we settled it."

Guess she doesn't want to talk about it.

Then she asks what I'm doing and when she'll get out of here. I tell her what I've learned and where I'm headed. Then I double-talk my way around the second question. People inexperienced with the legal system are not used to the slow grinding of its mechanisms.

She frowns, but then asks, "So you haven't found the prowler?"

"If it was just a random thief," I say, "we'd be very lucky to run across him, especially with no physical description."

"Then how do they usually catch them?"

"Burglars get caught doing another job. They'll have some items from the previous burglary stashed at their crib or in a storage locker. Or maybe they spend too much money or talk too much in bars or hangouts where the cops have people who tell them such things."

"But nothing was taken at our place."

"That makes it tough. Besides, you didn't see the person or know who it may have been. So we just have a shoeprint, a cigarette butt, and a thread."

"No fingerprints?"

"No, the lab guys couldn't get any off the pole. And we don't know of anything else he may have touched, except for the gun, of course. But they only found your prints and Morrie's on it."

"What about the killer's?"

"You touched it after him, maybe you smudged or covered his. Maybe he was wearing gloves. Could be he gave it a quick wipe down before he dropped it."

"So you're still just on a fishing expedition?"

"Actually, I'm searching for someone with a motive for threatening or killing Morrie. Maybe it *was* just a prowler who didn't know Morrie from Adam, but I'll work on the other assumption."

"But who would want to kill Morrie? Or threaten him?"

"I was hoping you might know. Oh, did you reach Minnelli?"

"What?"

"Louie Minnelli. You know, he called you the other day."

"Yes, I talked with him. He wanted to talk over some business matters. I told him I'd look for his records when I got out of here."

So he *was* the Louie who called her. She runs a hand through her hair, which looks stiff. She seems to be losing the glossy finish to her skin, hair, and nails; this place is no picnic.

"I was thinking about the night of the shooting," I say.

"What about it?"

"Do you recall if the patio door was open?"

"I'm sure we had it closed. We keep it that way." A spare smile forms on her lips. "One time I left it open, a squirrel got in the house, and Morrie freaked. I had to chase it out with a broom. He said they can have rabies." She shakes her head. "He was a real city boy."

"When he went outside that night, did he close it behind him?"

"I'm sure he . . . well, no, come to think of it, I believe he left it open a little. Maybe so he could get back in quickly, or call to me."

Darn, I must have a lousy poker face. Maybe I won't go to Vegas after all. At least to gamble.

"Yes," she continues, "I'm surprised he heard that noise outside, because it's pretty quiet with the door closed."

"Um hmm."

"I'll bet when the prowler dropped that pole, it made a racket."

"But you were able to hear the voices—"

"Because the door was cracked. Otherwise, I might not have."

Really. Time to switch horses in the middle of this murky stream. "I also wondered about the shot you fired at the man."

"What about it?" she says.

"You didn't call for him to stop? Yell that you had a gun?"

"No, I didn't yell. Morrie was lying there. I saw the revolver and heard a noise by the fence, so I picked it up and shot at the guy."

"Aimed at his head?"

"I'm not sure, but I think so."

"Did you consider shooting at his back? It's a bigger target."

"Maybe I did aim there. I can't recall. Really, I was in shock."

"But you're such a good shot, I'm surprised you didn't hit him."

"I pointed at a dark shape that was moving. That's not an easy target."

"But if you pointed at a man, why did I find the bullet

stuck in a tree ten feet above the ground?"

I see an intake of breath, but she moves on. "I squeezed the trigger as I stood up, so maybe I angled the shot too high. It happened very fast, so I'm not sure."

I'm going anaphylactic myself. Her story's crumbling, and I'm in this up to my bushy eyebrows. No golden parachute for me on this one.

"Okay, that's it for me. Do you have any other questions?"

Her face seems to harden. "I've got a hearing tomorrow afternoon. What do you think I should say?"

I'm not her lawyer. Or her conscience. "Whatever feels right."

Back in my Ford, I sit a moment, thinking about what I should do next. Then my cell phone sounds off. "Austin Investigations."

"*Oye, compadre,* I wanted to thank you for the lead you gave me." It's Sammy Tiburon in California. I don't get what he means.

"On Sleek Enterprises?"

"*Si, senor.* It was a winner. Better than a topless joint."

"How so?"

"It's a movie studio. Actually, an old office building that's been cleared out. They have lights, cameras, a bed."

"A bed?"

"The main focus. Naked bimbos hanging around waiting to film a scene or two. Couple of stud guys, too, but that's not my thing."

"They're making porno flicks?"

"Low budget, but a lot of gorgeous chicks get their breaks, or think they will, starting out 'acting' in these romp and fondle reels."

"I take it you asked a lot of questions."

"Everything I could think of. Two redheads and a blonde doing some wild scenes. You wouldn't believe what they did."

I don't think I'll ask. "Sammy, could you figure any connection between anyone there and Morrie Jacobsen?"

"One old guy here sets up the lights—been here eight years, lucky *perro*—said he remembered Jacobsen coming here three or four months ago. He and Morrie chatted a bit, while Morrie watched some filming and waited to talk with the head *honcho*."

"The lighting technician and Morrie talked business?"

"Nah, they gabbed about their mutual interest in big jabalonies."

Ah, perverts. A special fraternity. "So did you talk to the head guy, Lorenzo?"

"Out-of-town. Went to Vegas. He'll be back in two days."

"But the lighting guy seemed cooperative?"

"Sure, as long as he gets lunch money."

"Thanks, Sammy. I'm going to fly out there soon. I'll take a run at Lorenzo and the lighting guy, too. What's his name?"

"They call him Spots. Last name's McElroy. I gotta go back to my job, anyway. The rumor is Spielberg may be on one of the sets this week. Maybe I'll get my break and get hired on with the *jefe*."

"Wow. The boss of bosses. Break a leg, dude."

After a few hours at Vickie's, I've put together separate files for Sleek Enterprises, Bahama Mama Sales, Lugio Brothers, Minnelli Promotions, and Horowitz Enterprises. The deals with Lugio, Minnelli, and Horowitz look straightforward, aside from the late change by Morrie in not using

Charlie Greeb. But I don't understand his dealings with Sleek and Bahama Mama.

He received checks from them with lots of zeros on them, then sent them an invoice for items which didn't co-incide with his business inventory. This went on weekly for the past three months. Looks funky to me.

I review bank records, spotting a pattern. As I suspected, Morrie deposited funds to accounts in Switzerland and Grand Cayman in amounts close to what he received from Sleek and Bahama Mama. He was undoubtedly laundering money.

The accounts are under business names that are prob-ably shams, but I can't check them out. I'll drop in at the FBI office in town and run these figures past an agent. He'll know whether what I suspect looks feasible, and he can get subpoenas to trace the funds.

The big question I have is why Morrie got mixed up in this criminal enterprise. I presume he'd been a legitimate businessman in the past. Why the sudden foray into the realm of the underworld?

I drum my fingers on the desk and gaze around the room. I've searched the file cabinet, computer files, the desk. What more can I—

The closet. I've only glanced in to see if Morrie stored any boxes of records there. Seemed like it was personal items, sort of an overflow storage place for stuff you don't often use.

Still, I amble over there—my leg stiff from sitting for so long—open the door, and switch on the light. Looks like Morrie's stuff is on the left side of the closet. Vickie's clothes, boots, and old tennis racquets are stacked on shelves on the right.

Morrie put his stuff in boxes, labeling them with a

black marker. Income tax records. Old checks. A box of photographs, which I sift through, finding what looks like a recent photo of Morrie and Vickie standing outside the front of the house, knee-deep in snow.

I stick it in my pocket. The other photos seem to date as far back as a few years. I don't find anything that piques my interest or rings any alarm bells, just the usual shots of them on day trips around here. Here's some with them wearing heavy parkas, probably taken in Chicago.

There's not much on the carpeted floor, except for some Reebok sneakers. I kneel down and check them, finding nothing. Another box holds used golf balls, tees, a golf glove, and keys on a chain advertising Miller & Company. I close the box and get to my feet, hearing a squeak as I do.

It wasn't my knees or back or whatever creaks and cracks any time I move. It was the floor itself. I kneel back down on one knee, kneading and pushing at the carpet with my hand. I'm rewarded with another squeak when I press a spot that gives under the pressure.

I tug at the carpet at the back of the closet. It's loose. Yanking on it, I find a wood floor beneath, where I spot two bright brass hinges. There's a trap door about a foot square cut into the floor.

Well, Alice, let's see what it is. The door to wonderland? A portal to Hell? I pull it open, finding a cavity nearly a foot deep. There's what looks to be several large sheets of paper, folded into about a ten-inch-square, lying atop a shoe box. I unfold them and see they're blueprints of Morrie's project.

But why would he stash them here? I'll have to compare them for sure, but at first glance, they seem different from the blueprints I've looked at before. Now I see the date on them, which is about two years ago. The ones in Morrie's file cabinet were more recent.

I lay the blueprints aside and lift out the shoe box sitting in the hole. I set it on the carpet and open it. I'm not easily stunned, and I should have expected this, but I'm taken aback by what I see—a stack of photos that are shocking in their content.

I sift through them quickly. They seem to have been taken at various places with different cameras, some with a professional look to them, some obviously amateur photos taken in bedrooms. The principal theme is nude poses by young girls of probably eight to twelve years old. Some show sexual contact with older men, most fat, hairy, and balding. No men's faces shown. They're disgusting.

Some of the pics have white script initials in the corner: BM, which I'll bet is Morrie's business partner in Miami. I can't look at these anymore, though I might glean more information from them. But I've decided I should hop a plane to Miami to scratch around Bahama Mama's operation. Hopefully, I can put them out of business.

I put the lid on the box, place it back into the floor, and shut the trap door. Standing up, blueprints in hand, my knees crack. I pace back and forth across the room, trying to work off my edginess.

My cell phone sounds off. When I answer it, I'm surprised.

"You know about your client's hearing tomorrow at two?" says Detective Bagley.

I say that Vickie told me about it.

"I wondered if you'd found anything in your investigation that I don't know about? Anything that might be pertinent to the hearing."

I think of the bullet that's still in the back of my Expedition. "I did run across one thing, a bullet I found in a tree. I don't know if it was the one she fired at the prowler or not."

"We'd better do ballistics. Could you bring it by right away?"

I agree, but I wonder how he knew I'd found more evidence. Maybe he was only being thorough, but I'm a little uneasy about the timing. Unlike many investigators, I *do* believe in coincidence, and I dig the sparkle of serendipity, but still, it's a puzzlement.

Chapter 10

The sun rises up red and ripe into a cloudless sky. There's an easterly breeze, and the birds are in song. Such harmony of nature lifts my spirits more than psychotherapy or Prozac possibly could. I just hope my investigative vibes are in tune for my trip to gatorland.

Binga and I pee in the yard, sniff the air or the ground, then go inside for breakfast. I dress, then grab my carry-on bag. Lastly, I set out a heaping pan of crunchy dog food and a plastic bowl of water.

Stroking Binga's fur, I say, "I'm off to Miami, girl." Her liquid brown eyes seem to ask: You'll be back soon, won't you?

Tomorrow night, I tell her. She can sleep in her dog house tonight. She flops on the porch, probably thinking such is a dog's life.

Driving down the gravel road, I'm thinking that something odd was going on between Bahama Mama and Morrie. If I can analyze their agreement, maybe the motive for the killing will jump up and bite me. Poke around enough, and you'll often find the goodies. As long as you don't, bear-like, poke your nose into the wrong hole in the tree and get stung. Crooks, like bees, hate snoopers.

As I drive to the KCI airport, the photos Morrie kept in his closet pop into mind. He didn't deserve a tragic fate—we all have failings—but this case is giving me a bad taste in my mouth, and it's time to end it. I'd like to nab the killer, turn the mess over to the cops and the FBI, and return to my unity with nature.

At the airport, I pass through metal detectors without a peep, board the plane, and settle into a seat. I'm jammed between a small Cuban woman who doesn't speak English and a fat, bearded man who's dead asleep and snoring. As we fly across Middle America, I skim a travel book about Miami and practice my rusty Spanish with the lady. The man never wakes, though his snorts let several rows know he's still alive.

Now we soar over the Everglades, with miles of russet sawgrass and wetlands. There are some small green islands the guide book calls hammocks, sad in their isolation. And I see a mob of flapping white forms which must be snowy egrets, or wood storks, or white ibis.

Life subsists, even with no computers, faxes, or cell phones.

The plane drones over a city crowded with beige sky-scrapers and a heavy salting of creamy buildings and houses. Green dabs of palms wave a greeting. The captain announces our landing will be delayed, and he'll circle the area. It'll be nice to see the show.

We fly over Miami Beach, its white beaches beckoning the harried, with two cruise ships nodding like Loch Ness monsters in the chipped blue waters. Then South Beach, with bright white buildings trimmed in mint green, powder blue, and pastel peach, summoning the *avant garde,* assuring them that cool Art Deco is happening here.

Returning to the airport, we fly over green treed islands encircled by pink free-form shapes. A sculptor named Cristo calls them Surrounded Islands. They're stunning against the blue ocean background. The city has spunk, I hope it has answers.

As we descend, parched palms and bleached houses

seem bleaker up close. Everything looks seared, the area like a harbinger of global warming. Not that Kansas has heavenly weather, but still . . .

The terminal's a steam bath, the A/C defeated by muggy heat. Dodging distressed adults, playful kids, and piles of luggage, I pass through a roar of Spanish and English that makes me homesick for the quiet of my farm. My conversations with Binga are far less chaotic.

At a shop on the concourse, I buy a city map. Then I take off in a rented red Taurus. The Airport Expressway goes through Liberty City and Overtown, sectors much like old shoes with rundown heels.

Turning on the North South Expressway, I drive through Little Haiti, an area with the charm of a crushed tin can. Once downtown, I pass the Miami Arena, with the soaring Freedom Tower behind it peering out over the water, then on past the Bank of America Tower.

It's been forty-five minutes of fighting traffic, which moves like syrup through shimmers from the concrete. I'm approaching Little Havana and Bahama Mama's corporate HQ. My heart thumps faster.

The building's square and shabby. It's in a row with a few other businesses, five blocks from the ocean. Guess I'll take a stroll by it.

Out of the Taurus, it feels as if I've stepped into a bread factory. No moving air—stifling. One end of the building seems to be attached to the next business, a travel agency, with a door between them.

No one even sees me. The door's unlocked, and with a push, it swings open. The sidewalk becomes a brick path leading to others.

Each building in the block has one of these walkways, all ending in a covered concrete pavilion sporting a red-tiled roof. Looks like a soda fountain island in the middle. About twenty people sit at the sheltered tables, sipping drinks, some smoking cigars or cigarettes.

Next I take a stroll around the block. Next to the travel agency is *Jaime's Servicio de Automoviles,* a car repair shop. The overhead doors are closed, so I poke my head inside the entrance. Men in overalls hunch over cars, doing body work, cutting torches tossing sparks, and—

"What can I do for you?" says a heavy-shouldered Hispanic, wiping his hands on a red rag.

"My ride needs some repairs. I haven't seen this place before."

He stares at me a little too long, then says, "Anyone send you?"

I shrug. "Nope, I just came on my own."

"We're busy. Can't get to any new jobs for a couple of weeks."

"It shouldn't take long. Maybe you could work me in one day."

He shrugs his shoulders. "We're all tied up. You'd better go somewhere else. I got to get back to work."

"No problem." The cars being worked on are expensive models. Not the type of vehicle you'd expect to see around here.

My recon continues. Next is *Garcia's Cigarros,* and around the corner rests *El Mundo Restaurante,* a meat market, and *Rodriguez Periodicos,* or magazines, mostly in Spanish. At the rear there's an open-air vegetable market, a beauty parlor, and a barber shop standing side-by-side. On the far side is a large building with a small sign saying *Almacen General,* or warehouse, and a filling station.

It seems the buildings may be patterned on the way they build businesses in Cuba. Or maybe it's a takeoff on the plazas often found in Hispanic towns, where businesses surround a central gathering area, usually with a park-type setting. Whatever, it seems it'd work pretty well.

But it's time to check out Bahama Mama Sales.

It'll be best to talk with an executive. I step into the waiting room among heat-weary, bored men slouched into black vinyl chairs. They give me a desultory glance, then go back to staring at dog-eared magazines.

I show the Cubana at the switchboard my PI license and ask to see Jerry Parmontal. She frowns at the license, and I'm reminded I'm now in the minors. She hands it back as though it were a wet taco.

"Do you have an appointment to see Mr. Parmontal?" she says.

"No, but it's important. I'm sure he'll want to speak with me."

"He's out of the office. I don't know when he'll return."

A dark-haired man in his thirties, wearing a guayabera shirt, shows his narrow face behind the receptionist. "Can you call Rivera for me, Katerina?" Spanish accent, Cuban, I'd guess.

"*Por seguro,* Senor Parmontal," she says.

We exchange looks; he seems to realize that I look out-of-place here, like a pig at a pool party. "Who are you?" he says, then looks as if he wishes he hadn't, because, plainly, he doesn't care.

"He's looking for Jerry," the receptionist says.

"He's out. Come back *manana,*" he says, and starts to turn.

"Mr. Parmontal," I say, stopping his move. "I'm a private investigator here on a serious matter. Could I speak with you?"

His mocha-colored eyes are set in a rather handsome

face that's spoiled by a sour expression. They seem to smolder. He looks as if I offend him.

"I'm busy," he says, as though that will end our contact.

"Then I can wait awhile. I flew here to see you."

He rubs his cheek, his eyes showing he can't believe this pesky fly hasn't yet been shooed away. "I'm busy all day. Geraldo might be back later. *Tu puedes esperar . . .* you can wait for him, if you want."

"Maybe I could catch him, wherever he is. It won't take long."

His lips edge into a smile, but the look gives me a chill. He smoothes his slick hair. *"Por seguro.* That would work *muy bien."*

He gives me directions to a gym called *Punos de Acero.* After closing the door, I can hear Parmontal and the receptionist chortling.

Having forgotten my English-Spanish dictionary, I'm working on the gym's name. *Puno* means fist. But I can't recall the word *acero.*

After finding a parking spot, I hobble to the front of the dingy business. Drawings on the windows show figures of men kicking and punching each other. It's a karate dojo. *Punos de Acero,* I realize, means fists of steel.

I earned a brown belt in Tae Kwon Do in one of these places, but then hurt my back and never made black belt. Still practice some basic kicks and punches on a heavy bag in the barn, but with my numb left leg, I can't make many moves. Not to mention having slowed down.

As I enter the place, the familiar smells of sweat and tension hit my nostrils. A bored-looking teenager behind a small desk glances at me, then returns to reading his martial arts magazine. In the foyer, plastic chairs line one wall, magazines cover a scarred table, and pictures on the walls show youngsters and adults sparring or breaking boards.

On a stand near the desk are a bunch of trophies with the usual figure atop them of a guy doing a side kick. They're for sparring contests and kata, or form. Some are sizable, and I check them out.

One's for first place in sparring in a Florida state contest. The biggie, which I move to see the engraved plate, is for first in sparring in last year's Southeastern Karate Championships. Both awarded to Jerry Parmontal. As I move the tall trophy back, I spot something near the base, examine it, then move the trophy to the front.

"Jerry Parmontal here?" I ask the torpid teen.

He glances up from his magazine. "Look in the workout room."

"What does he look like?"

The kid gawks at me as if I blew in from Kansas. He jerks his head toward the wall. "His picture's by the door. He owns the place."

In the photo, Jerry looks to be six feet tall, maybe thirty-five. He resembles his brother, but he's stockier. Looks limber in the roundhouse kick he's throwing in the picture; he's hit his sparring partner in the head.

The workout room features white-gone-gray mats covering the floor, dingy walls with drawings, and floor-to-ceiling mirrors. A dozen young men grunt, throwing kicks as instructed by their sensei, Mr. Jerry of the lightning foot. They're brown belts, mixed with some black. Jerry's got his third degree black belt. Impressive.

The circular clock on the wall shows a couple of minutes to the hour. They'll probably break up soon. Sure enough, he calls them into a line facing him; they bow, then head for a door, probably to shower.

He turns, padding toward me like a panther. When he

spots me, he slows, sizing me up as all fighters do. I don't feel comfortable with the look he's giving me, though it's not hostile, just guarded.

"Can I help you?" he says. He stops about six feet from me.

I tell him that I'm interested in Morrie Jacobsen.

The light goes out in his eyes. Moments ago, he looked catlike, but now has a snake's blank stare. Hope he's not planning to strike.

"Take off your shoes and come in," he says. "Class is over, and I think well in here." As I shuck my shoes, he says, "But I don't know anything that'll help you. In fact, I just heard that Morrie was dead."

"Who told you?"

"A guy in Chicago who worked with him." He stops in the center of the mat, turns, and gestures for me to sit, then lowers into a cross legged squat on the mat. Comfortable for him, the prick. I get down and cross my legs, stiff as hell.

"How did you hurt your leg, *hombre?*"

He must've watched me in the mirrors and noticed my limp.

"Car wreck," I shrug. "It doesn't bother me much."

"Slows down your karate moves, I'll bet. *Que mala suerte.*"

Yes, bad luck, all right. "How did you know I took karate?"

"The way you move, even with the limp. Your feet grip the mat, comfortable with the give of it. Some guys come in here, they bounce around on it like it's a . . . what's that springy thing?"

"A trampoline?"

"*Exacto.* So what's your question?"

Down to the grit. "What were your dealings with Jacobsen?"

"I'd have to ask my bookkeeper. I didn't know him too good."

"You're in different businesses, and yet, you sent him large checks every week for several months."

His eyes narrow, and he resembles his acerbic brother. "I don't know what you're saying. I do business with *todo el mundo, sabes?*"

Everyone, yes, I know. "So can you tell me about the particular transactions with Jacobsen's company? I have copies of canceled checks. We can talk to your bookkeeper or whoever might know."

He rises straight up, as though he had pistons propelling him. I clamber up, my numb leg feeling like a fence post.

"I run this karate dojo, Bahama Mama, and a bar. I'm busy. I'm sorry Morrie got killed, but I don't know nothing about it."

"One thing," I say, pushing my luck. "Did he owe you any money when he died?" Parmontal's last check to Morrie was never offset by a deposit to the Swiss account.

He looks perturbed. Probably both at Morrie and at me. If his brother were standing beside him, they'd look like mean twins.

"I don't see that . . . no, I don't think so. Even if he did, that's somethin' for my lawyer to work out. I had nothing to do with Morrie dying, so I guess you might as well go back to Kansas."

Did I say I came from Kansas? The PI license has the state on it, but he didn't look at it closely. Anyway, his saying he had nothing to do with it just convinces me more that maybe he did.

Okay, I have a temper. And I don't like getting the

bum's rush out of a place. Ask me nicely, and I'll go, but if not . . .

"I could show you copies of the checks," I say, "and maybe it will jog your memory. They were big ones, I bet you'll remember."

"*Mira* . . ." he says, pressing close to me, our chests a foot apart, "I mean, look, I don't want to see no fuckin' checks, I don't want to talk about Morrie no more, and I don't want you hangin' around here. *Comprende?*"

Oh, yes, I believe I understand. "That's fine. Maybe those lawyers you spoke about can work something out. Maybe you'll even get to come to Kansas to tell a judge about it."

I turn to leave, stopping at the edge of the mat to slip my shoes back on. As I get the second one snugged in place, Parmontal just can't help himself, and he shoulders me, bumping me into the wall.

"Oh, *perdoneme*," he says. "I thought you were leaving."

I give him a hard look. "I am. Don't push."

Boys being boys, he just has to brush me again. But he makes the mistake of coming too close. I push my finger into the spot just below his larynx, and he takes a step back and grabs his throat.

"*Adios,*" I say, heading through the doorway. Then I feel him grab my jacket sleeve. As he turns me around, I throw up my left arm to deflect the punch toward my head, but he follows it with a straight left to my solar plexus, which knocks my wind out into the street.

Doubled over, I watch his torso. He draws his leg back to deliver a side kick into my body. Lurching to the side, I whip both arms across my body much like swinging a golf club, which deflects the kick so that he grazes my thigh. Otherwise, he'd have broken my leg.

From my position against the wall, I consider my options. I could grab him—I took judo and know FBI defensive tactics. But he's stronger and in better shape, so it'd just be a matter of time before he wore me down and pounded me.

Out of the corner of my eye, I see the trophies. As he recovers his balance and starts after me, I flip one off the stand. It crashes to the floor, pieces breaking off and skittering across the linoleum. He suddenly reminds me of Robert DeNiro in *Raging Bull*, his eyes full of hate and fury.

"*Cabron!*" he yells. "Don't you touch . . ."

He goes stiff as I touch the top of the biggest trophy, then topple it as though it were a pool stick that slipped from my grasp.

As I'd hoped, he lunges for it, trying to make the old diving catch. And, I'll give him this, the guy's damn fast. He gets one hand under it, juggles it for a couple of seconds, gets it under control—

And I step in with a straight right punch to the temple, then put the heel of my hand against his chin and shove his head back as I sweep his left leg out from under him. He goes down and smacks the back of his head with a crack on the hard floor. He lies there, dazed.

Predictably, the trophy smashed to the floor, knocking off the base and scattering white powder all around. I step over the guy and nod to the skinny kid whose mouth is hanging open. "Better give him a hand," I say.

I wait on the sidewalk for a couple of minutes, wave down a passing cop car (who said they're never around when you want one?), and tell him there's a man with cocaine inside the karate place.

The cop looks at me oddly, but kills his motor and heads inside. I clamber into my rental car. That's enough excitement for the day; I'm ready to return to Kansas where people have better dispositions.

But now I'm wondering what's going on at Sleek Enterprises, the other company that sent Morrie suspicious checks. Think I'll check it out. Maybe sunny California won't be as torrid as Miami.

Chapter 11

Tired and battered after my scuffle with Parmontal, I think that rather than battle traffic back to the airport to catch a redeye flight home, I'll just stay here overnight. Maybe eat some dinner, watch a movie on TV, then get a good night's sleep. I head for the Biltmore Hotel, which is out of my price range, but it's close and so huge they'll surely have a vacancy.

As I drive up I'm impressed by the statuesque tower that my travel book says was modeled after the Cathedral of Seville. Valet parking, doorman, bellhops. This is going to cost a bundle.

Once inside my spacious and luxurious room, I'm glad I came. You only live once. Wish I could telephone Binga, but she's yet to get her own cell phone, so going for the next best thing, I punch in the number for Amy Harrington. She's there, and I'm glad; I ask about Vickie's hearing.

"It went about as expected. They had nothing new and startling, but she was bound over for trial. The good news is the judge lowered her bail. She thinks she can arrange for the money."

"When's the trial?"

"No date was set. We have motions hearings in three weeks. I'll try a few standard moves, but nothing's going to get her out of trial unless you come up with proof that someone else shot Morrie."

"Hope springs eternal. I'm working on some potential baddies."

"Really? You must be as good as I've heard."

"Don't believe courthouse rumors."

"We'll see. So what've you got?"

"It's pretty tangled up right now. Give me a few more days to work through the knots, then I'll drop in and lay it out for you."

"All right, Mr. Tightlips, but I was sort of hoping we could see each other, you know, get together and discuss the case soon."

"That's a fine idea, Counselor. I've got to do some more traveling, but as soon as I light back in Kansas, I'll give you a call."

"We could have dinner here at my place. Contrary to all indications from my tough lawyerly manner, I'm an excellent cook."

"And I'm a wizard with corks, so I could bring a bottle of bubbly, if you like."

"You know the way to my heart."

"Oh, how's Vickie's eye? You know, where she got hit?"

"It's purple, but she's okay. You should've seen the other gal."

"What happened, anyway? Vickie wouldn't tell me."

"You know how jails are, Max. Some tough butch thought she could run over the pretty new fish and get some extra dessert. Of course, that would've only been the beginning."

"So Vickie put up a fight?"

"Did she ever. She told me later that when she was in college there was a serial rapist terrorizing campus, so she took a self-defense course. She liked it so much that she took jiu jitsu for another three years."

Jeez, I'm beset by a plague of martial artists. Kung Fu hell. "I'm glad she's all right."

111

"She's fine. And Carla has a cast on her arm where Vickie twisted it and tossed her to the floor. She's saying she slipped."

"That happened to a guy I met here today."

"It happened . . . Max, you're not getting into any rough stuff, are you? Jesus, I know you're in shape, but you're a little past—"

"Say no more, you're right. I've already told myself everything you're going to say. I'll try to keep a civil tongue in my head."

"I hope so. Is there anything else you can share with me?"

"Let's just say that I may be sniffing around the right tree."

"Is this like the tree you found the bullet in?"

"Sorry about that. Do you think that hurt Vickie's chances?"

"Hard to say. It was another log on the bonfire they're building to roast her backside. Anyway, if you get a suspect, tell me ASAP."

"You'll be the first to know. It'll give me an excuse to call."

"I've been wondering why you hadn't."

"Sorry, I guess I'm rusty at the rituals."

"That's rather endearing. Call me when you get back, and try to come bearing circumstances of mitigation or exculpation."

"Are you worried?" I say.

"When you add the life insurance policy and the bullet you found high in the tree to the smoking gun, blood on her hands, and a pending divorce for infidelity, I'd have to say things look grim."

"Just lucky she has such a talented lawyer."

"And a hard-nosed investigator. Have a safe flight."

And the line gives me that old, familiar hum.

What do I do to offend people so?

I splurge and enjoy a great dinner of grilled tuna with a glass of chilled Chardonnay at the Kaleidoscope restaurant in Coconut Grove. I'll have to eat peanut butter for a while when I get back to the flatlands, but so what? The palate should be indulged on occasion.

As I approach my room, my cell phone vibrates in my pocket. Strange, I wasn't expecting any calls. The only person in this area I gave my number to was Marisol, but she's working tonight.

I punch the answer button, then stick the card in the door lock. Technological wizard at work. Sure enough, it's her.

"Hey, I thought you were working."

"I am, Max. I'm sitting on a wiretap. But I need to tell you something."

She sounds serious, which is out-of-character for her. Maybe she's just busy and can only talk briefly. "Sure, shoot."

"We've got intercepts on Parmontal's phones. Did you see him today? He made some calls, and he sounds mad as hell."

"We had a short chat. He didn't care to cooperate, then he got pushy. Anyway, I thought he'd be in the slammer."

"Hell, Max, he's got all the local cops in his pocket here, you should know that. He's not going down for a small possession rap."

"He had to have several keys of coke in some trophies there. Maybe more in the back somewhere. That's a lot to us Kansas folks."

"Just a little hill of beans here, besides, there's the protection. Anyway, he's been dialing Vegas. I think he's arranging a hit on you."

"What? I can't believe it."

"He didn't say it exactly. He might settle for you to get handed your ass by a couple of tugboat-sized thugs. Just watch your back, *amigo,* we can't have such a *guapo* guy get his mug messed up."

"I can't believe he can't take a knockdown without whining."

"He's got a rep for being hard. Real macho, *tu sabes.* I guess you made him look bad in front of his boys."

"He started it," I whimper.

"I'm sure. Oh, there's a call on my machine. Take care, *cunado.*"

What do you know? This is stranger than the mysterious neutrino. Catch a flight to Miami to sort out information on the case, and I end up in a hazardous asteroid belt.

Surely no one followed me from the dojo. At least, I didn't spot anyone, and it probably would've been too soon for them to start a tail. There's no way for them to know I'm staying here, except that I'm registered under my true name, so they could find me if they called all the hotels in the area.

Nah. I'm just getting paranoid. Seen too many gangster movies.

Speaking of which, I'll check tonight's movie schedule, try to find a good flick to get my mind off this dilemma. Ah, *Chinatown*, with Jack Nicholson. Haven't seen that in a few years. Then there's some action ones with Jackie Chan or Bruce Willis.

Of course, I could watch something more sedate, such as *Fried Green Tomatoes, One Flew Over the Cuckoo's Nest,* or

Hamlet, with Mel Gibson and Glenn Close. No, come to think of it, there's murders in all of those. I'm surrounded by killings.

Hope that's not an omen, such as the eclipse of the sun right before the earthquake in Turkey. I'd hate to die in Miami and be fed to the sharks. Who wants to sleep with the fishes?

Anyway, I watch *One Flew Over the Cuckoo's Nest*, then brush my teeth. As a precaution I check the door, putting on all the locks. Then I plump my pillow, switch off the lights, and settle into bed.

But this pillow might seem more comfy with a Colt .45 under it.

After paying all that money for a big, comfy bed, I slept fitfully all night, rolling out several times to check noises in the hallway outside my door. Half awake, I dress, eat breakfast, then check out. The attendant brings my car, so I don't have to worry about a bomb hooked to the ignition, unless it's got a delay switch or a device like Dennis Hopper used on the bus in *Speed*.

But since I don't have Sandra Bullock to drive for me while I check the undercarriage, I'll have to take my chances. Besides, the movies portray people operating much more efficiently than they do in real life. Such as the flick *Enemy of the State*, in which the NSA uses cameras and satellite images and computer hookups to follow and analyze their target's every move. Sure.

The true world is filled with mishaps, foul-ups, and flubs. I think I made one in my contact with Jerry Parmontal. I gave away more information than I got, which is a cardinal sin in any investigation.

But I did pick up a clear signal that this alien bunch in

Miami was tied to Morrie. Otherwise, my sending probes into their area wouldn't scramble their signals so much. And they wouldn't be sending a Death Star after me.

Or maybe I'm getting melodramatic.

At the airport, I make it through security, then settle in my seat for the return flight to Kansas. I'll bet my blood pressure drops thirty points. Before I fly to California, I'll stop at the house to check on Binga.

A dark-haired young man beside me whispers into the ear of a gorgeous girl with light brown hair. She giggles, then gives him a loving gaze. They look as though they're returning from their honeymoon. Ah, young love. Ah, love at any age. Hard to beat. For a minute I reflect on everything I know about love and relationships.

As the plane zooms up into the troposphere, I recline in my seat, eyes closed, thinking. I had an odd dream last night. It involved our solar system, with the nine planets orbiting the sun.

Jupiter soared majestically through space; Saturn, with its marvelous rings, whirled about like a debutante at a ball; and Mars cavorted with abandon as it glared with fierce red eyes. The array spun with clock-like precision and balletic grace.

There was confusion, too. Comets, asteroids, and meteorites whizzed through the solar system. Huge flares leapt from the sun's blazing corona; the solar wind spewed electromagnetic particles in every direction. With all the chaos, I found myself standing outside in my yard not knowing where to point my telescope.

Why such a dream?

Okay, maybe the fiery meteorites and shooting stars are symbols of the array of conflicting facts I've found in this case. And my confusion hampers my ability to focus my investigative scope, causing me to miss the organizational hub I should have seen. Maybe Morrie was an errant satellite to a system that went haywire and had to be destroyed before he damaged the whole network.

Yes, I've got to visit Culver City and Las Vegas to see if I can make some sense of the orbits of the various players in this peculiar dark galaxy, and, hopefully, to find the center of it all.

My place looks just as I left it, and Binga cavorts about the yard, happy as a furry clam to see me back. I'm glad she doesn't know about the evil force I met on my trip, I don't want to upset her.

I call a travel agency and book a flight to Los Angeles tomorrow. Binga will be peeved; she's not accustomed to my jetting all about. We've been exclusive here in our own little world, and I suppose I like it that way, although I still enjoy human contact when it's available.

Here, off the highways and byways, there's a feeling of remoteness and safe harbor. We're away from the clamor of city streets and the frantic activity of a metropolis. It seems impregnable to evil; I hope that's the case.

I'm tired, but there's something I want to examine this afternoon. I give Binga a big snack, then as she seems ready for her afternoon nap, I tell her I have to go out for a while. She gives me a look, then flops down.

Vickie's house is quiet, and everything looks undisturbed. In Morrie's office, I pick up the blueprints from his cubby hole in the floor and the ones from his filing cabinet drawer, and take the works to a table in the sunroom. First, I study the blueprints Morrie stashed with his dirty pictures. They seem like plans for a pretty standard industrial park, with quite a few buildings, some storage, warehouse space, etc.

Then I unroll the other ones. They're more recent.

The configuration looks different from what I've just examined. Even more so than I thought. There's a large central building, then walkways to a number of satellite buildings which are of various shapes, with a few names etched in, such as auto shop, main office, copy center, warehouse areas 1, 2, and 3, and sleeping quarters.

Sleeping quarters in an industrial park? Sounds new to me. But maybe they were trying to make it like a truck stop, too, because there's a place marked "restaurant." All the comforts of home.

And there's another set of prints which seems to entail a schematic system for computer stations. I don't understand this, but it bothers me. I realize every business, large or small, uses computers these days, but still, in an industrial park?

If there's one thing I learned when I worked in the FBI, it's that you should enlist the help of experts when you can't solve puzzles. In this case, I'm thinking of Jim Barber, a young agent who works in the FBI office downtown. He's a whiz with computers.

I punch in the phone number from memory. Contrary to general opinion, my mind's often as sharp as a new razor. Well, one that hasn't been dulled by scraping against too many grainy problems.

Jim answers. He's surprised, but pleased to hear from me. I haven't been to coffee with the guys there for a while, but promise I'll drop by soon, and we chat a bit.

"Max, I've got a hearing in an hour, and I need to get some stuff together. Let me know when you're coming down."

"I did have one problem, Jim."

"What's that?"

"I'm working a murder case—the developer, Morrie Jacobsen."

"I read about it. You hitting some bumps?"

"Same old rocky road. There's some blueprints I had a question about. You could probably decipher them easily, if you'd take a look."

"I'll be glad to. When could you drop them off?"

"I'm flying out tomorrow. I can bring them by the office now."

"So I can look at them yesterday?"

"If that's a convenient time for you."

"What the hell. Bring 'em down. If I've already gone up for the hearing, just slide them under the door."

"See you." As per a country song, I put the pedal to the metal and make it in thirty-two minutes. I press the intercom buzzer beside the heavy metal door with the bullet-proof glass inset. Jim bounds out of his office, jacket on and tie cinched. Must be going to the hearing.

"Hi, Max, I was just going upstairs. What've you got?"

I spread the blueprints on a desk. "These are the plans for Morrie Jacobsen's latest project out east of town. There's some symbols and configurations here I don't understand."

He glances at the top print. "I think I can follow these. Anything I don't understand, I'll run by this architect I know. We'll get it deuced out for you." He checks his watch. "I'd better hustle. Good to see you, man."

He locks the heavy inside door, then the thick entrance one. Turns the cameras and security alarms on. All in all, it's a secure spot. At least, I thought it was until the day the guy came into our building tossing pipe bombs and firing pistols all over the place. That's when you begin to muse about your mortality.

Chapter 12

Descending into the San Fernando Valley, the San Gabriels looming to the north, with the jutting buildings of downtown L.A. choked in brown mist, I imagine slipping downward into Dante's above-ground inferno. What a place to build ten-million-dollar mansions. Men's values often escape me.

LAX throbs with people, and I scan the mob for celebrities. We create our own deities, although I don't value some of our newer "stars"—those of the hard bodies, vapid minds, and scant acting abilities. The folks reared on TV don't realize that a seasoned character actor can add the spice that makes a movie palatable.

In my rented Skylark I struggle through traffic that reminds me of salmon thrashing upstream. Taking Sepulveda Boulevard north to Culver Boulevard, I then follow it into Culver City. After winding around a bit, suddenly Sleek Enterprises appears. I'm underwhelmed.

As Sammy Tiburon said, it's no more than an old two-story office building, tones of mud brown and dog barf beige. But as I park, I see there's more to the picture. Ambling around a bit, I find there's a compound of buildings built to coordinate with one another.

Inside's a tiny waiting room which you might find pictured in a massive dictionary under the word "seedy." At a battered desk sits a receptionist. She's all Hollywood: big blond hair, big blue eyes, big—

"Can I help you, sir?"

"I'd like to talk with Spots McElroy, please."

"He's working on a shoot right now."

"Maybe I could just slip inside and catch him on a break." I lay a bill on the desk where General Grant can stare at her big—

"Of course, sir, that'd be fine," she says, scooping up Ulysses and stuffing him down her low-cut top. "But promise you'll be quiet, sir. They don't like to waste film doing retakes."

"You have my word."

So I slip in, finding myself in a murky space that resembles a school auditorium with no seats. There's a series of lights on poles, all focused on a bed. An old guy wearing a battered ball cap, years' worth of cigarette-induced wrinkles, and a bored look adjusts a small spotlight on the crotch of a naked, indifferent young woman.

Sitting behind the camera is a guy in a black beret. He must be the director, cinematographer, and, probably, the producer of this proud cinematic achievement. He's telling the muscled and motivated male actor to resume his position, which ends up being imaginative, if not acrobatic. Then he says for the kid to prepare to "act."

The girl yawns, then transforms her face into a grimace of pain and pleasure. Sure, easy for her. But who carries the real load for this performance, huh, ladies?

The director/cinematographer/producer says "Action," starts the precious film rolling, and gets another three-minute shot of salacious sex into the can. All in a day's work. Art for art's sake.

He yells "Cut, print," to nobody's surprise, adding, "Let's take ten. Charlie, get the blonde with the skunk tattoo on her left—"

"Monique?" asks Charlie.

"Whatever." He turns away to study his "script," which is a wire bound spiral notebook with handwritten notes in it.

Charlie lumbers off to fetch Monique of the famous tattoo, and I slide over to where the old guy's fiddling with a light stand.

"Hi," I say, "are you Spots?"

From the cigarette stuck to his lips, smoke curls upward into his eyes, and he blinks as he tries to see me. "That's what they call me."

"I'm just a movie buff, but I'd say you got a nice lighting setup here. That last scene should photograph rather like the effect in *Cat on a Hot Tin Roof*, with Newman in a sweaty bed with Taylor."

Now he straightens, takes the fag from his mouth, and regards me as more than stage scenery. "Yeah, 'Maggie the Cat.' That's a fair comparison. It wasn't no *La Dolce Vita*, or *From Here to Eternity*, but I was going for what they used to do for Kim Novak." He takes another drag, drops the butt, then grinds it out on the linoleum floor.

"The gal in that scene," he says, blowing out plumes, "has character in her face, or maybe just good cheekbones, but I tried to emphasize it." Then he adds loudly, " 'Course no one around here knows enough about movies to give a shit." Beret Boy looks up.

"Could I buy you a soda, since you're on a break and all?"

He casts a look of disdain toward the director, nods, and says, "Why not, no reason to come up with anything new around here."

As we leave, the director says, "Except for the actors."

The guy's more on the ball than I thought. I turn and nod to him. He goes back to reading his script.

There's an alcove with a pop machine and a candy machine and a large urn of brewing coffee with Styrofoam cups stacked beside it. I feed quarters into the pop machine, we grab our soft drink cans, then we sit down in chairs at a small table.

Spots takes a long drink, lights up another Camel, exhales expansively, then says, "You're a cop, ain't you?"

"Do I look that typecast?"

He laughs, broken-voiced and gruff, the sound coming apart into moist phlegm. He stands and spits into a trash basket, takes a drag, and says, "Jesus, I gotta get off these weeds one of these days."

The guy's pushing seventy. When?

"Actually, I'm a PI. I'm from out-of-state, too. So I'm no threat."

"I ain't worried. But you been a professional cop, huh? You got that look about you."

"You don't miss much, Spots. Got the eye. I was FBI for twenty-five."

He takes a solid nicotine hit. Must not be the day to quit. "I thought so. What kind of movies do you like?"

"For me, it was always mysteries and westerns. Probably because of the action. And there were some films that used good lighting effects in the mystery genre, like *Chinatown*, or *L.A. Confidential*."

"Sure," he says, "and *The Postman Always Rings Twice*, *Dial M for Murder*, and *The Manchurian Candidate*."

"Even westerns," I say, "like *High Noon*."

He grins, showing small, dingy teeth with their own layer of film. "You know somethin' about movies, all right."

"I'll bet you used to work on some good ones," I say, guessing.

He stops in mid-inhale and stares at me. Brown eyes, a bit bloodshot. "How would you know that?" he says.

"You seem to know what you're doing. What happened?"

He lays his ciggie in a flat tin ashtray. "Long time ago I got in a beef with a director. He had some ideas that stunk up the film as far as the cinematography, but he didn't care for me sayin' so."

"And he was powerful enough to keep you from getting work?"

"Back then he was. He killed himself five years ago. But by then I was pretty much washed up, anyway. Two more years, I'm retiring."

"So, how is it for you making porno flicks?"

"No challenge, 'cept what I invent for myself. It's sorta like when Marlene Dietrich and Greta Garbo had the pot lights, you know, the small spots showing their faces off. Except I'm supposed to skip the head and concentrate on places from there on down."

"Tell me that's all bad, Spots."

He goes into another laughing, coughing spasm, his face reddening. "Pal, you got me there. Still, it gets dull. I used to try low-key lighting and low-angle shots. Now we do an establishing shot, mostly use high-key lighting for everything, and don't much screw with different angles. The actors do that for us."

And I have to laugh. After taking a long pull of my Diet Coke, I set it down and pull a photograph from my coat pocket. It's the one of Morrie and Vickie.

"Spots, do you recognize this guy?"

He looks at the photo and nods. "Yeah, this's the guy another PI was asking me about. It's that Morrie. He was here a few months ago. I shot the shit with him while he was waiting to see Carmine."

"Lorenzo, the head of the studio?"

He smirks, his mouth toying with a laugh. "Okay, call him that. He tries to pay the bills and keeps the bimbos flooding in."

"You saying there's not good money in this racket?"

He waggles a thin hand. "That's not it. There's some coin to be made. But there's a lot of fingers in the pie, you know?"

"Like silent partners?"

"Yeah, they're silent, except when they show up for their cut. You ain't got it, they're like a atom bomb blowin' up your ass."

I nod. "How about—"

"By the way," he says, "who's the woman?"

"The woman?"

"In the photo."

I look down at Morrie and Vickie, side-by-side in Technicolor, one of them still living. "That's Morrie's wife, Vickie. Why?"

He waves a hand dismissively. "Nothin'. I just thought she looked familiar, too, but I can't place her."

"Hmm." I toy with my soda can. "Do you know what connection Morrie had with this place?"

"Not really, but I'd say Carmine had him in his pocket."

Spots and I saunter back to the set. Charlie's jawing with Monique, who has the identifying tattoo thrust at him. A new leading man stands by at the ready; the other actor must've petered out.

I ask Spots if this place was ever used for other businesses.

"Sure, it used to be an independent film studio. They come and go around here. They had a couple of flicks that made some money, then a string of flops that dried up the dough, so they folded."

"Anyone else use the place?"

"Some aeronautics company had it for a while. They merged with a bigger fish, most everyone got fired, and they closed down." He gazes at his light bars, eager to start fiddling. "Anything else?"

"That's it." I shake hands, slipping him a hundred-dollar-bill. "Let me buy you lunch for your trouble."

He sticks it in his pocket. "No trouble, I like talkin' movies with someone that knows where he's coming from."

"You going to feature that skunk tattoo, or put it in a shadow?"

He looks at the girl with the pictorial, silicone-enhanced boobs. "Hell, she went to all that trouble, I'll light 'em up like the Hollywood sign."

"Hooray for Tinsel Town," I say, and stride off, as Beret Boy, perched on his canvas sling throne, stares at me strangely.

Time to try my luck with Carmine Lorenzo, the head of this sleazy establishment. The receptionist doesn't seem put off by my request to meet with the Great One, though I sense hesitation before she buzzes him on the intercom, as though she thinks I'll stuff the other side of her bra with more filthy lucre. I won't, as she'll soon find out.

"He's on the phone," she says. "I'll buzz him when he's off."

"That's fine," I say, turning toward the grubby chairs hugging the wall, but with no intention of sitting. Instead, I examine a wall filled with photos of young actors and actresses, some framed, some stuck up with cellophane tape, a few autographed. There's a quality in those unlined faces and bodies—a hopefulness captured in crisp 35 mm film.

I don't recognize any of the faces or names, and some of the photos have no identification. At least, the actors aren't in the buff, attesting to the studio's good taste. Many are wearing bikinis or swim briefs, as though they were taken poolside at a private dunking grounds. A poor man's Hugh Hefner act. Class C movie moguls in action.

The actors are a healthy-looking lot. Bright, capped teeth glowing in handsome and pretty faces. Suntanned and buffed physiques. But some of them seem tarnished or frayed around the edges, revealing they've already had a taste of the hard life.

And now I spot a familiar face. I think. Or am I imagining this?

It's not a close-up shot. The guy is tall, dark, and in his late thirties. He's with two babes, with his arms around their shoulders and hands drooping to their breasts. I can see the face well enough to be pretty sure it's him. But why is Louie Minnelli on this wall?

The photo of him that Phil Emerson sent me from Vegas is in the car, so I can't compare it here. The receptionist answers the phone, and I decide the hell with it. I pull the snapshot from the wall and slip it into my pocket.

The receptionist hangs up, then punches a button on the console. After a short conversation, she hangs up. She gives me a big smile and says, "Mr. Lorenzo says you can come right back."

I start toward the hallway, pause, then dip into a pocket for my last Grant engraving. I lay it down, saying, "Thanks for your help."

It goes into the crevice to join its companion. "Mr. Lorenzo says he's got to go to a meeting, but he'll give you five minutes."

Ten dollars a minute. Expensive interview. But I wink at her as if to say she did her best, then head down the hall to an open doorway.

He's a swarthy man of about forty, around five-foot-eight, heavy build. Bright yellow shirt with dark chest hair showing, and, though I can't see his feet for the beat-up desk, I'd give odds he's wearing white loafers. He's clenching an unlit stogie in his teeth.

"Mr. Lorenzo?"

He motions me in and indicates I should sit in one of the faux leather chairs fronting his fortress-like desk. The carpet's worn and cheap. As I situate myself, he asks, "What's this all about?"

I introduce myself, show my credentials, and shake hands. His grip is tentative and perfunctory. Just like a kiss where you don't quite hit the lips.

"I'm investigating a murder in Kansas," I say.

"So why'd you come to L.A.?"

"To talk with business contacts. The victim was Morrie Jacobsen."

"Who?"

I hand him the photo of Morrie and Vickie. He glances at it, then tosses it back in my direction. "Don't know the man," he says.

"Jacobsen Development Company?" I say. "You corresponded with them for the past few months. Checks were sent."

He's shaking his head before I finish. "Don't know nothin' about it," he says. "Listen, I got a meeting I gotta get to right—"

"Here's a copy of one of your company's checks," I say, tossing it on his desk. "Made out for big dollars. Has your signature on it."

He regards me as though I were a member of the Smut Patrol. Bushy eyebrows lower over flinty brown eyes. "I don't know nothin' about any of this. You don't unnerstand English, or somethin'?"

"I don't understand why you're hiding information."

He pushes a button under his desk. "You'd better go now."

"What did Louie Minnelli have to do with this place?" I say.

"Don't know him either."

"His picture's on the wall in your reception room." Well, it was.

"Half of L.A. is there. Don't mean I know him. Hey, boys . . ."

I turn to see Charlie, the fetcher of tattooed ladies, and another guy standing in the doorway, looking like two well-fed steers.

"Yeah, boss?" Charlie says.

"This guy's on his way out. Make sure he—"

"Thanks, Lorenzo. I'll call you," I say. I pace toward the two hulks blocking the exit. This will be like shooing coyotes, you take them head on and watch them scatter. Unless they're like two grizzlies who'll tear me apart.

Lorenzo says nothing. The two men ease back just enough for me to squeeze through. I say goodbye to the receptionist, and leave.

Outside, the sun having burned off the smog, the day seems clear and pure. Maybe it's a result of having escaped that studio. Seems as though there's a residue of slime clinging to my skin.

There's a black Mercedes parked by a sign saying it's reserved for C. Lorenzo. I ease by the front passenger door. Some papers are on the seat, but it's hard to make out . . . ah, I spot something: a valet parking ticket for The Mirage Hotel in Vegas. So, Alice, this is getting curiouser and curiouser.

For a while, I cool my heels in my car until finally Spots

comes out. He heads for an old Chevy Blazer, and I yell at him. He waves, and waits for me to cross the street.

When I reach him, I hold out the Vegas mug shot of Louie Minnelli.

"Recognize him?" I ask.

His brow wrinkles. "Yeah, he used to help run things around here. Louie . . . Louie . . . I can't remember his last name."

"Minnelli?"

"That was it. He didn't do much except hustle the talent."

"When did he leave?"

"Oh, musta been about five, six years ago. Somethin' like that."

"And he went to Vegas?"

He hands back the photo, saying, "Naw, to Chicago."

"Chicago?" Now I'm puzzled. "Are you sure?"

"Yeah, I remember him grousin' about how he was gonna freeze his magic wand off up there after gettin' it warmed up so good here."

"Charming."

"I don't remember much about him except that he was a real turd."

The kind that could float to the top in a certain kind of business.

Chapter 13

Taking Jefferson Boulevard toward the airport, I decide to eat at the Roll 'N Rye restaurant, a classy deli with comfy booths. I order a corned beef sandwich and a Löwenbräu. While I wait, I check out the art hanging on the walls. Shortly, the waitress arrives with a sky-high sandwich and an icy cold beer. This isn't Iowa; maybe it's heaven.

As I munch, I think about the case. Something's going on here that I don't understand, much as many of the workings of quantum physics are still beyond my grasp. But there's got to be a design, with all the people I'm running into seeming to be connected.

The waitress stops back by and says, "How's the corned beef?"

"Wonderful," I say.

"Better have another brew with it."

I hold out my arm, and she gives it a twist. It's for a good cause; I'll be taking another flight soon and need to settle my nerves. But back to my entanglement theory.

I'm assuming a group may be involved here, and I'll try to chip away to see which people belong. Then I'll fall back to study the big picture and see if I can make any sense out of this world within a world. Next stop, Las Vegas, and I hope my luck will be running hot.

Full as a goat at a tin can factory and lubricated with German beer, I turn in my rental car at LAX, then book a flight to Las Vegas, leaving in an hour. Headed for Glitter Gulch and the Strip. Yee haw.

The flight is short, with barely time to eat my tiny bag of peanuts and drink half of a Diet Coke. I'm sitting close to first class and can hear the popping of corks and experience a vicarious thrill.

Maybe someday I'll win the lottery or hit it big at Vegas or win a Nobel prize and spend the rest of my days in luxury. I'll take world cruises, dine at five-star restaurants, and attend cultural events at Kennedy Center. Or maybe I'll just laze around at my country place reading books, searching the heavens with my telescope, and playing with Binga. Given the choice, I'd have to think it over long and hard.

Dusk is falling, and we're gliding downward toward the City of Glitz. It seems to be in the throes of a forest fire, but as we swoop lower, I see that the brash glow is from millions of lights that glint, glimmer, and glare, summoning prey to the sticky core of the various casinos. Ah, the majesty of gaudy taste and frivolous architecture.

All this to get people to gamble? What a waste.

According to the papers and most of the FBI agents I talk to, the iron grip of La Cosa Nostra in Vegas, as well as in other cities, has eased to the mild press of tin foil. Most of the tough bosses of the past are either dead or in prison. The criminal syndicates have splintered and fallen apart.

But seeing this garish neon jungle sure makes me wonder.

I take a limo to The Mirage. As I viewed it from the air, its two massive wings flanking a taller center structure, I thought of the Phoenix rising from the cinders, or in this case, from the sands of the desert. And as the limo approaches it, I note the top layer of the high rise gleams a radiant gold in the slanting sunbeams. How symbolic.

I called Phil Emerson from the airport; we'll meet in a bar at The Mirage. I said I had a surprise for him, thinking of Louie Minnelli's photo from Sleek Enterprises. Perhaps he'll have other info that'll help piece together this batch of confetti-like clues.

After checking in, I set my bag on a dresser, then head back to the elevator to meet Phil in the bar. Sidling into the medley of hoarse laughter, clinking glasses, and shared tales of woe, I blink my eyes against the hanging cigarette smoke, then spot Phil sitting across the room at a small table. He's nursing a beer and smiling at a stacked platinum blonde two tables over.

Some people never learn.

I plop down across from him, saying, "Good thing I got here in time to douse you with a glass of water before your pants catch fire."

He grins, takes a sip of his beer, and signals a waitress to come put us out of our misery. "I'm just keeping in practice, Max. Nothing serious. Hell, flirting with the babes is what makes my job bearable."

"What'll you handsome gents have?"

"Another one of these," Phil says, tipping his bottle toward the waitress, then holding out his hand in my direction.

"Two, please."

"Coming up," she says, winking, then heading for the bar, swiveling through a pack of beefy car salesmen, dentists, and Shriners. At least, those are the conventions being held here.

Phil's grinning. "So now who's staring at what?" he says.

"Never mind. You got anything new for me?"

"Kimberly Walters, the hooker who was with Jacobsen and Minnelli the night the other hooker got smacked, works for a pimp."

"So she probably won't tell me diddly."

133

"That'd be my guess. He'll tell her to shut the fuck up."

"Unless I can catch her by herself."

"Even then, she'll be too scared to talk."

"Maybe. How about Minnelli? Anything new on him?"

"Just rumors. Like he's part of a young bunch of made guys who are planning to kick out the Mustache Petes and take over."

"He's got that much muscle?"

Phil shrugs. "He's always been a big talker, but he's not that high in the outfit. He's mostly an enforcer, not a planner."

The waitress comes back, dips, and sets the beers on the table. Phil tosses her a five as a tip and has her add the beer to his tab.

"Thanks," I say, raising my bottle. "To solving crime." I down a slug of cold brew, which tastes as good as icy water from a tin can after a game of summer baseball. It's dry out here in the desert.

I drop a photo on the table. "I saw this picture of Minnelli at Sleek Enterprises in California. It's a porno movie studio. Guy who works there said Louie used to be around about six years ago."

"No shit." Phil straightens his blazer, shooting out his cuffs. "I got no scoop that goes with that. You think it's a mob operation?"

"I got that impression. Nothing much to base it on except that Sleek Enterprises and a place called Bahama Mama in Miami were both sending checks to Morrie. Then he'd make similar deposits in numbered accounts in Switzerland or the Cayman Islands."

Phil shakes his head, his lips pushed out. "Money laundering?"

"Looks like it to me. I'm going to give it to the Bureau

to see if they want to trace the funds."

"But how does that help you in this case?"

"It doesn't, unless I can prove Morrie was working for this bunch, then figure out if something went wrong that'd make them want to whack him."

Phil gives a low whistle. "You think this could be a mob hit?"

Why does it sound so preposterous when he says it?

After some more cold ones we get up to leave the heady atmosphere of the bar for the even headier stratosphere of the casino floor. Phil makes a detour by the blonde's table and jots down her phone number. Some guys.

As we saunter through the crass splendor of commercial gilt, the sound of whirring slot machines in our ears, I ask what he told the woman to merit such immediate success.

"Just the truth," Phil says with a crafty grin, "that I'm investigating an international crime syndicate, but that I'd like to see her once it's resolved."

"How you do go on."

Just then a portly lady next to me lets out a whoop, and I jump about six inches. With her fists clenched in the air, she does a little jig in front of a slot machine that's pouring money over the top of the tray. Sporting Kmart's latest chartreuse slacks and a purple-patterned jersey top, her new white tennies gleam as she does a shuffle dance on the colorful carpet.

"Harriet!" She calls to a lady in a print dress. "I hit three sevens! My God. Must be ten thousand dollars rollin' outta there."

There *is* an impressive flow of silver gushing forth. People have gathered around, watching the woman and Harriet scoop up the riches in plastic cups and buckets. A dark, muscular man in a tailored suit appears at the edge of the circle of onlookers. My muscles tense.

"Congratulations, madam," he says, detracting her attention by his hard good looks and imperious manner. In a louder voice for the crowd, he says, "The Mirage is the home of more winners than any other casino. Your good fortune is our pleasure. Please come again."

She cackles like a hyena in heat and takes a step toward him. He looks startled, as though he's worried she might try to hug him. But she simply extends her hand and says, "You bet I will, mister. This is the best time I've ever had in Vegas."

I shoot a glance at Phil, who nods once, then we watch as Louie Minnelli shakes her hand, smiles, then melts away into the larger ambience of bright lights, vivid colors, and clinking chips.

"Wait here a minute," I tell Phil. I fall into a surveillance pace behind Louie, not looking at him except in passing as I scan the action at the tables.

Louie stops at a door, turning his head for a last inspection of the activity. He shoves it open and vanishes through the private exit. I stroll around a bit more, then circle back to meet up with Phil.

"Let's go up to my room," I say.

"You got an angle to play?"

"You can bet your alimony check."

Phil and I get comfortable in the large room. He folds his blazer and lays it on the king-size bed. I toss mine on a chair and kick off my shoes. We sit at a small table, each laying out papers and notes.

We bought some soft drinks and snack food on the way up here to help diffuse the alcohol bubbling through our bloodstreams and brains. Intent as I am on solving this case, I must admit I'm feeling mellow. I bite into a chocolate frosted donut, sip a Diet Coke, then address the work before me.

As I rummage through my briefcase, spotting the mug shot of Louie Minnelli, I get a cold fish feeling. Surely this low-level mope in a maundering crime organization in Las Vegas can't have anything to do with a murder in Kansas. But the fact that he and Morrie were arrested together does eat at me.

"Phil, can you think of anything else that might tie Louie into this case? I'd like to get him into my net or toss him out. At this point, he's tangling everything up."

Holding a palm up, he says, "Nothing I've run across, but I know an ex-agent who works security here. He might have an idea."

"Can you get him up here?"

"Can the showgirls in Vegas put their legs behind their heads?"

I presume that means yes.

He steps over to the phone, makes a call, and after a short conversation hangs up. "He'll be up in ten minutes." Then he punches in another number and orders two Chivas Regals and water.

"You're drinking again?" I ask as he sits back down.

"Naw, that's for Tim. He likes to have an occasional blast."

Like the limousine driver for Princess Di. I'm not sure of the reliability of such a person. But, different strokes for different folks.

And as I open the door minutes later, I can't help but brush aside my preconceptions. Tim Pennington is one of those people who assaults all your senses at once, knocking you back on your heels as he strides into your life. He's about five-foot-six, bushy red hair, with cheeks and forehead sprinkled with so many freckles it reminds me of the Milky Way. A ten-kilowatt smile glares above a purple shirt with contrasting red, green, and yellow tie.

He sticks out a freckled hand, and we shake. As I feel his grip, I notice the muscles bulging against the shoulders and sleeves of his jacket. He pumps my hand like he's hoping to draw water.

"Hi, I'm Tim. Phil told me all about you. We worked together in Los Angeles about a century ago, did he tell you? I can get away for a few, then I gotta get back to the salt mines. Did those drinks get here yet?"

For a moment I'm stumped as to how to answer. Or even which question to answer. I start to ask him to come in, but I'm too late, as he's already breezed past me and struck up a conversation with Phil. I look down the hallway for the room service guy, but see no one, so I close the door.

Phil looks up at me and grins. "Now you've met Tsunami Tim."

"Nickname?"

"Yeah, one of the gals in L.A. laid it on him."

"Like the huge wave rolling in from the sea," I say.

"Huh?" Tim looks puzzled and a bit crestfallen.

"Tsunami," I say. "A tidal wave created when an earthquake hits under the ocean."

"Son of a bitch," Tim sputters. "All this time I thought it was Hawaiian for big wanger."

"You wish," Phil taunts.

There's a knock at the door. A young man's holding a tray with two hefty Scotches. He sets it down, and I grab my wallet and pull out some bills. Before I can return to the table, Tim has consumed half of the first drink.

"You have to be back soon," I say, "so I'll be brief. I'm working a murder case in Kansas, and it might be connected to some guys in Vegas. Mostly, I'm interested in Louie Minnelli and his cronies."

Tim takes another slug of Scotch and nods. "Minnelli could be into anything, including murder, but I don't know of any ties he has to Kansas. He's got connections in Chicago and Detroit, I hear, and he talks about L.A., but I don't know what he did there."

"I met a guy says he worked in a porno studio. Six years ago."

Tim finishes off the first Scotch. "Sure you guys won't join me? I feel stupid drinking alone. Not that I'm gonna quit, but I'll feel bad."

I raise my soda. "We hit it earlier. I'm trying to come down."

He shrugs and sips at his drink. "I'm not surprised that Louie would be involved with porno stuff, I just never heard about it. He does think he's a big ladies' man, and to tell the truth, he does pretty well. Of course, in Vegas you gotta be a big loser not to score."

"Know anything about his bust with the hooker who died?"

"What I read in the papers, plus a little scuttlebutt around here."

"What's that?" I ask.

"That it might not have been an accident."

"Ah. Did you know the guy who was with him that night? He's Morrie Jacobsen, the murder vic in Kansas."

He takes a hit of Scotch. Loosens his tie of clashing colors. Then he says, "I don't recognize the name. You got a photo?"

I go get the snapshot of Morrie and Vickie posed in the snow, which I toss on the table, trying to avoid the wet drink circles.

He stares at it a moment. "No, I don't think so. He doesn't look familiar, although I see about ten thousand faces a day, so you have to consider that in the old equation. But I'm pretty sure I haven't seen him with Minnelli, for what that's worth."

Phil says, "You see a lot of Minnelli?"

"Sure, he's got a suite here, and he passes by our door going to the private elevator in the back. We got cameras everywhere, anyway, so I'm always spotting him out on the floor. But you know what?"

"What?" I ask.

"Now that I think about those back elevators, it reminds me where I think I've seen this woman."

"The one in that picture?" *Déjà vu,* over and over again.

"Yeah, the cute gal in the snow with Morrie."

"That's Morrie's wife, Vickie."

"Whatever. I never heard her name and never met her. But I'm pretty sure I've seen her with Louie in the last few months."

"I thought you saw ten thousand faces a day," I say.

"But not all this hot. Some things stay in my head longer."

"You didn't see Morrie with them? Maybe he was here with her, and they were just meeting Louie for a drink."

"Like I say, Louie does okay with the broads. It didn't look like they were going to meet her old man. They were real cuddly."

Phil cuts me a glance. "Could be a connection. Like you were looking for. Maybe we should check—"

"Of course, I may be wrong about this," Tim says.

"How's that?" I ask.

"In this picture she's a blonde." He hands it back. "The woman I saw with Louie was a redhead. A colorful redhead, with a fine ass. If you had a backside photo of her, I could verify her in a second."

A breast man in Culver City; a butt man in Vegas. Sex always rears its ugly head in my cases. Too bad it doesn't come up in my personal life.

"I don't think I have any such pics," I say. "But Morrie's wife has been a blonde for the past few years."

"Damn," Tim says, then downs the last of his second Scotch. "She sure looks like that gal I saw pawing on Louie."

"But then," Phil says, hand upturned, "everyone has a double."

"Not me," Tim says. "I'm empty, and I gotta get back to work."

Tim walks away as steady as a Volvo on the interstate. I'd be weaving all over the carpet. The man's a world class guzzler.

As I close the door, Phil says, "So what do you think?"

"Damned if I know. The deeper I get into this, the less I understand. It's like our telescopes showing us ever more of deep space, but we don't know enough about what we're seeing to determine how it affects us."

Phil's eyes bug. "What the hell you talking about?"

"Cosmology. I've been looking into it the last few years."

"And I thought I was deep when I learned about astrology."

"Phil, I think we're off on separate paths there."

"Maybe, but I bet mine works better with the chicks."

"Undoubtedly so."

"So what are you going to do?"

"Only one thing to do: I'll talk to Louie, see what he tells me."

Chapter 14

Tsunami Tim told me that Louie Minnelli eats breakfast in his room, then about ten o'clock begins to wander around the casino floor. I've been waiting near the private elevator in the back of the casino since nine. Now it dings, and the door slides open. Louie and another guy who looks like a giant turnip in a tight suit amble out.

I move toward them.

"Hi, Louie, remember me?"

He halts, adjusts his lapels, and twists his neck in the tight collar on his dark blue shirt. His tie and fancy leather shoes probably both cost more than my suit. Turnip Man moves toward me, but Louie holds up a hand, freezing him. "No, I don't, pal, who are you?"

"We haven't really met, but we talked on the phone when you called Vickie Jacobsen. And I've seen your name in Morrie's records."

I note a glimmer of understanding in his eyes, but he tries to mask it. "That don't mean nothing to me. Who are you?"

"Max Austin, PI, working on Morrie's murder case."

"Why would a private eye do something like that?"

"Vickie's lawyer hired me because Vickie's a suspect."

He shakes his head. "She'd never do anything like that."

"So you know her well?"

He adjusts a shirt cuff. "I didn't say that, I just—"

"But you know how she'd act."

142

"Look, I talked to her a couple times when I did business with Morrie, and she seemed like a straight lady."

He glances at Turnip Man, who reads some signal and moves forward like the lead blocker for a high-salaried running back.

Before the blob can get in my face, I blurt out, "You got arrested with Morrie, and you were seeing Vickie. What was going on?"

He holds up a finger, and the vegetable halts.

"Seems like you're butting into my personal business," he says.

"A PI can be quite a snoop. I also learned that Sleek Enterprises, where you once worked, was laundering money through Morrie."

He stiffens, making him a good two inches taller than I. "Sometimes snooping in the wrong places can be real dangerous."

"So I've heard. Especially on hokey TV crime movies."

He nods at Turnip Man. "Let's go, Buster."

Now Buster does get in my face. I hope he doesn't have the bad taste to shove. Oh, damn it, there he goes.

He pushes against my chest, and I clamp his hand there, then grab his wrist and twist it as I pivot. This forces his arm straight, elbow up. He leans down to ease the pressure on his wrist and elbow, I press my weight on his arm, and he goes to his knees.

Louie's complexion is a shade of purplish-red, and he shouts at the hapless veggie, "Shoot him, you idiot."

I don't like fighting two guys, at least one of them with a gun, so I cut the odds by straightening up and kicking Buster in the temple, knocking what sense he had right out his ears. He slumps to the floor.

"You son of a bitch!" Louie remarks.

Then, as I'd hoped he wouldn't do, he reaches inside his jacket about shoulder holster level. As I see the blue metal object emerge, I lurch into him, pinning the gun to his chest before he can point the bad end in my direction. Better safe than sorry.

"Let's just stay cool, Louie. No one has to get hurt."

As we struggle, he sputters, "Go fuck yourself."

I shove him backward, slamming him against the elevator door, conking him a good one on the back of the head. As he blinks and relaxes his grip on the pistol, I wrench it away from him, drop the magazine from the weapon, and rack a cartridge out of the chamber.

"I'm leaving now, Louie. Don't expect to see this pistol again. I suspect convicted felons aren't supposed to carry such things."

Louie blanches, then stares at me, not moving. But I hear a sound behind me, and turn my head in time to see Turnip Man come to his feet, gun in hand. Why did I have to unload Louie's piece?

The barrel pointing at my face seems the size of a cannon.

Louie says, "Take him upstairs and do him."

I swallow hard. But just then I see a red blur arrowing toward Buster from behind. There's a crash that makes me wince.

Buster grimaces, jerks upward, then twists to his right and doubles over in pain. Tsunami Tim hit the old Turnip right in the kidney. He must've been a linebacker.

Tim takes Buster's gun, and the wilted veggie slinks into the corner to whimper. Louie looks apoplectic. I grin big time.

"You haven't heard the last of this," Louie says.

Can't these mopes come up with any original lines?

★ ★ ★ ★ ★

With no regrets, I check out of The Mirage. I thank Phil, and tell Tim I'm sorry if this jeopardized his job. Louie threatened to fire him.

Tim smiles and says, "Hey, after you left I told him I'd keep working here until I found something else. I said a new job would make it easier for me to forget that he tried to kill an obnoxious PI."

So now all I have to do is track down a hooker.

Phil drives me to Kimberly's last known address, an apartment building at the fringe of the Strip. I ask him to wait in the car, so she won't feel overwhelmed by lawmen. She's in apartment 3B, so I hike up the stairs for exercise. The climb makes me pant like Binga.

Knocking on her door feels strange, and I expect to see some old lady in curlers stick her head out of another apartment, giving me a reproachful glare. I'm just here to get information, lady. Honest.

I sense eyes on me, probably from the peephole, then the sound of a couple of deadbolts being withdrawn. She's not too careful about who she lets in. Maybe I look like a client.

She's younger than I expected, probably stretching it to call her eighteen. Don't they have any laws in Vegas about this sort of thing? She pushes thick, dark hair out of her pretty baby face, her brown eyes dim from leftover drugs or lack of sleep.

"You Social Services or a cop?" she asks.

"Close," I say. "Could we talk a minute?"

"I'm sleeping. Come back later." She starts to close the door, but I slide my foot into the doorjamb position. Old habits die hard.

"This is important, and it'll just take a minute."

She glares at my foot, then sighs deeply and says, "Come on in. Make it quick, I gotta get my sleep. I got a guy coming over at five."

She switches on some lamps. Each time she leans toward the light, her firm, slim body is outlined through her silk nightgown. I can see why guys like Louie and Morrie might give her a call.

She melts into a catlike position on a teal-colored velvet couch. I flip open my credentials to show her my PI card. She shrugs.

I sit, then look into her eyes. "I'm working a murder case. A guy you saw a few months ago, Morrie Jacobsen, got killed."

Blank look. "That long ago, I don't remember nothing. Forget about names."

"Here's his photo," I say, showing the one of Morrie and Vickie.

She glances at it. Recognition gleams in her eyes. She's silent.

"He was with Louie Minnelli," I say. "You were with your friend, Tiffany. It was the night she died."

Now her eyes mist up. I guess the other girl *was* a friend.

"I sorta recall him. Don't know nothing about him, 'cept . . ."

"Except what?"

"Not much. He had a temper, like all guys."

I'll bet she's seen a lot of that. Maybe starting with her father.

"I need to know what happened that night. It might help me in the murder case I'm working."

"I told my story to the cops. That's all I remember."

"I saw your statement, but I was in the FBI awhile, and I know sometimes people recall more than what they told the cops. Especially later, after they've thought about it some more."

She hands back the photo. "I don't remember nothing more than what I said. Now I gotta get some sleep."

Handing her my card, I say, "If you think of anything, call me collect."

She takes the card, holding it limply.

I open the door to leave.

"Who the fuck're you?" asks a tall, skinny guy who's holding a key. He's dressed in black, with an open-collared shirt and a thick, silver chain around his neck. Huge silver rings dwarf his bony fingers.

"Max Austin," I say. "Just here on business, but I'm leaving now." I slip through the doorway and pace toward the stairs.

"Hold on a fuckin' minute," he says.

I pause.

"Who that muthafucker be, Kim?"

She comes over to stand beside him, stroking his arm. "He's no one, Cobalt. Just a private dick. Nothing to do with us."

"What you tell him?"

"Nothing. I didn't have nothing to tell. Anyway, it wasn't about you or me, just some john from a long time ago."

He smiles at her, then includes me. Silver front tooth.

"They's been a lot of them, huh? Hard to recall one guy."

"Well, I remember the . . ." Then she stops, her eyes getting big. She knows she screwed up.

"No, bitch, you don't remember nothin', like I said." He shoves her, and I stiffen, heat creeping up the sides of my neck.

"We won't be seein' you no more," he says, slamming the door.

I blow out a breath and clench my fist. There's a thump and a woman's screech. Followed by more smacks, crying, muffled moans.

None of my business. I'm getting in more fights over this stupid case than I've had in my whole life. If I go busting in, it'll just be worse for her later. The guy's probably armed, and he might shoot or stab me or Kimberly. Best to walk away when you can't really help.

But I did cause her pain.

Striding back to the apartment door, I try the knob, finding it locked, then bang my fist against it in a lawman's demanding clamor. I stand to the side of the door, which is standard procedure, but which seems to make even more sense because I'm sure the Turkey in Black is holding heat. Bullets zipping through a door can still hurt.

But there's no fusillade of lead. And the painful sounds of fists on flesh stop. Then the door flies open.

"What?" He looks at me as though I just peed on his parade.

"Just so there's no misunderstanding," I say, "I wanted you to know Kimberly's being straight. She told me nothing."

He stares at me, fiddling with his chain.

"So," I continue, "there's no reason for you to be mad at her."

Now he's nodding and giving me an insincere smile, like a crocodile. "Fine of you to tell me. Now get the fuck out of here."

He slams the door shut. Almost. It bounces off the toe of my shoe, back into his face, and I add to the momentum by throwing my shoulder against the wood.

The Man in Black stops the door with his forehead. He staggers backward, looking dazed, and flops onto the bed.

But even in his stupor his autonomic nervous system functions. He dips into his pocket and comes out with a knife that'd cut off a hog's head. I don't like facing long, sharp blades, so before he can thrust it into any of my vital organs, I throw a right hook to his jaw.

Now I'm thankful for the extra ten pounds. It gives my punch enough authority to knock the Man in Black with Big Knife colder than a clam on ice.

Kimberly's face goes as white as sugar. "Oh, shit," she says as she clambers onto the bed and pats Cobalt on the cheek. "Look what you done."

"He may be out for a while," I say.

"Oh, shit," she stresses.

"Will he be mad at you, or will he just want to gut me?"

She quits patting him. "He'll cut both of us up and feed us to some fuckin' piranhas he's got in a tank at his place."

These guys definitely watch too many B movies.

"Oh, that old trick," I say.

"Why'd you do that?" she asks.

"I didn't like you getting hurt."

"Can the bullshit, you just . . ." She's staring into my eyes. "You're telling the truth, ain't you?"

"Best I know how."

Then she startles me as much as if a shooting star had whizzed through the window. "You know, that's the first time anyone ever cared what happened to me." A tear dribbles down her cheek.

I help her off the bed and put an arm around her. "I'm sure that's not true, Kimberly. But, listen, you've got to get out of here."

"Oh, God, you're right." She wipes her eyes with the

back of her hand, stares at her business partner, then digs in his back pocket and comes out with his wallet. She cleans out the cash and drops the empty billfold on his skinny chest.

"He owes me," she explains.

"I'm sure," I say. "Can I drop you somewhere?"

"The airport. I gotta put some distance between me and him."

"I was just going that way," I say.

Kimberly takes five minutes to dress and throw clothes, jewelry, and shoes into a suitcase. Cobalt starts twitching, so I relieve him of his knife. Outside, I slash a tire on his shiny Camaro, then I jam the blade into another tire, jiggle it until air whistles out, and leave it stuck there as a memento.

Phil drives, with Kimberly and me scrunched down in the back seat. Tires squealing, we beat it for LAX. On the way, Kimberly tells me she'll return to Minneapolis. "Maybe I'll get a beautician's license," she says.

Crying, she says the life was brutal and she's glad to get out.

I tell her I'm happy for her.

After some silence, she says, "You really working on a murder?"

I nod. "Morrie Jacobsen got shot. As I said, he's one of the guys with you the night Tiffany went after Minnelli with a knife."

"That's not what happened," she says.

I look at her; she seems different. Sort of like a Midwestern girl. Softer, more trusting, and honest.

"Would you tell me what *did* happen?"

She gives me a tiny smile. "I think I owe you that much."

"I don't want to get you into more trouble."

She laughs. "As they say: 'If they can't take a joke, fuck 'em.' "

"There's nothing you'd have to testify to, but the information might point me in the right direction."

"Like Polaris showing true north?" she says.

I stare at her a moment. "Why do you say that?" What a crazy world we live in. Aliens everywhere.

"I saw the zodiac signs on your watchband. Figured you were either into astrology or astronomy."

She should apply for the FBI. "Good observation. Impressive."

"A girl has to notice things. Look for danger signs and all."

"Can you fill me in on the night with Minnelli and Jacobsen?"

She takes a deep breath. "Okay, here's the deal."

By the time we reach LAX, she's told me details which change the story. Tiffany didn't go after Minnelli with a knife, as I already suspected. In fact, Minnelli was with Kimberly. Morrie had Tiffany.

"That guy . . . Morrie? He liked young girls. Tiffany looked younger than I do, so Morrie picked her. We dressed in short skirts, cotton panties, pigtails, you know, the schoolgirl look."

Charming. "So what started the fight?"

"I'm not sure; maybe Tiffany said something wrong. We were supposed to talk like little girls. Morrie got pissed off if we didn't."

"So Morrie got angry with Tiffany?"

"Really pissed. First, he slapped her, then she got mad and started tellin' him off, and that made him even hotter. I told her to chill, but it happened too fast to stop."

"What did?"

"Morrie punched her, grabbed her by the hair, and swung her around, knocking stuff over. She screamed, and he choked her."

"He strangled her?"

"No, maybe he would've, but it didn't get that far. Tiffany had a bad heart. She turned pale, grabbed her chest, then just collapsed."

And now Kimberly sobs hard, letting it take her over, as though she's denied herself this time of grief until now.

"We tried to wake her, but couldn't. Someone banged on the door, and Minnelli came out with a knife. I thought he might stick me, but he said, 'Listen, Tiffany got mad at me and pulled a knife. We wrestled, I smacked her, then she had this fuckin' heart attack. There's ten grand in it for you.' "

"Who was at the door?" I say. Though I already know, it's a good way to check whether she's telling it straight.

"A guy saying he's an off-duty cop, and he heard noise and came over to check it out. He looks at Tiffany, then calls 9-1-1."

"You got your payoff?"

"I didn't do it for the money. If I'd crossed them, they'd have killed me, too. Minnelli don't fuck around. But he paid me, all right. Tiffany was dead. Nothing I said or did would've changed that."

"I see what you're saying. Thanks for telling me the truth."

We pull up to the boarding area for American Airlines.

"I'd better take it from here," she says.

"Sure," I say, and smile hopefully.

We look at each other a long moment, then she hugs my neck hard. "Thanks for saving me, Max. But we're all even now."

"Totally square. Good luck, Kimberly. Have a good life."

"If you're ever in Minneapolis, look me up. Helen Crandall."

"Sure thing, Helen." I watch her stride off into a new world.

Phil twists in the front seat to look at me. "Did she help you?"

"Infinitely."

Chapter 15

When I land in Kansas City, I walk off the plane feeling as tired as an overloaded mule. Jet lag, they say. Dehydration. Or maybe walking two miles in a crowded terminal lugging a suitcase. And I still have unfinished business.

Back in Hillsboro, I stop at the jail. Need to ask Vickie a couple of questions. Once I go home, I'm sure I'll flop for quite a while.

The guards buzz me through various iron gates, and I head for the prisoner interview rooms. Two of them are empty, and I wait at the middle door. The guard escorting me, who looks as though he does a lot of bench presses and sandwich lifts, stares vacantly for a moment, then says, "No, not that one. Go in Room C."

I'll go along to get along, but I'm not in the mood to be hassled.

"What's the difference?" I say. "They're both the same. Both empty."

He shrugs. He has no neck. "They said to put you in room C."

Sighing, I trudge over to the other room, sit down, and wait.

Within minutes, the guard delivers Vickie, then slams the door. Bits of dust drift down from the ceiling and land on the table top. I adjust my chair, then open a notebook and click my pen.

"I just got back from L.A. and Vegas," I say, watching for a reaction. There is none. "I'm trying to find suspects in Morrie's murder."

"Are you having any luck?"

"These things build. I've got a good foundation."

Her eyes narrow a bit, as though she's judging the bullshit factor in that. I'd say she got a pretty high reading.

"I need to ask you something personal," I say, forging ahead.

"That's fine; I don't mind, if it'll help you. What is it?"

"Did Morrie like porno? Pictures, movies, Internet stuff?"

She pales, but doesn't falter. "I don't think so. No more than any man who likes to see naked women. Would you say you don't?"

"I'd plead *nolo contendere*." Should I ask if she knew Morrie liked hookers who dress as little girls? Maybe.

"Were you aware," I say, brushing a piece of dirt from the tabletop, "that . . ."

Then something hits me. I brushed bits of grit off the table the first time I was here. In this same interview room.

I look up at the ceiling light fixture. It's secured by two screws.

Vickie's staring at me strangely.

Putting a finger to my lips, I say, "Shhh."

Tumblers have fallen into place: bits of grit, being guided to a certain interview room, the cops knowing about the bullet in the tree.

Up on the table I climb, then pull out my keys and work at a screw with the edge of a metal FBI emblem. I manage to loosen it, then pull down the edge of the cover. There's a tiny microphone.

I tighten the screw back and climb down. More bits of grit settle atop the table. Just a guess, but I don't think the jailers put the mike in. But why would the cops do it? Still, they seem to know what was said here.

"When do you expect to get out of here, Vickie?"

She looks at me questioningly, but I nod.

"Probably tomorrow, or the day after," she says.

"All right, then I'm going to make copies of the records I need and keep them at my place so I won't be in your hair anymore."

"Whatever you want to do."

"So give me a call when you get out."

Thoughts are spinning in my head in elliptical orbits, like the planets in our solar system, with two fringe ideas interweaving like Pluto and Neptune. I want to investigate the recorder in the interview room, and I'd like to check out a theory I have about Vickie. Both might be part of the cosmological system I'm addressing. Or maybe I'm trying to create a parallel universe.

The easiest dilemma to resolve would be the relationship between Vickie and Louie, and whether it had any bearing on Morrie's murder. Maybe it was just a fling. And it's based on an identification of Vickie by Tsunami Tim from a photo I showed him. I know that an ID from a photo, even by an ex-FBI agent, can be unreliable.

I stop at Vickie's house. May be the last time I'm here alone, so I'll make the best of it. First, I make copies of all crucial documents. That done, I shift into phase two of my operation.

Back to the closet, but this time I sift through Vickie's side. The clothes in here are mostly sweaters, wool pants and skirts, and fall and winter coats. Guess she hasn't had need for them yet.

Nothing in here rings any bells. I should've asked Tim what Vickie was wearing when he thought he saw her in

Vegas with Louie. He probably wouldn't have remembered, anyway. Men aren't too good at that sort of thing. Hmm. I sound like a femi-Nazi.

But I feel more like a frustrated male as I poke through seemingly endless boxes crammed with old nail polish, half-empty bottles of hand lotion, lipstick tubes, perfume sprays, skin cleansers—all the bric-a-brac that constitute so much of the feminine existence. The money spent on such junk must be enormous. Unlike the money men spend on essential equipment for hunting, fishing, and golf.

There are two boxes back in the corner which look like old-style hat boxes, but I haven't seen any hats around. The first box holds a collection of gloves, woolen scarves, and knitted caps. There's even a couple of pairs of earmuffs—holdovers from Chicago, I'll bet, although I've seen it hit thirty below in Hillsboro.

In the second box are silk scarves, compacts, and some small beaded purses. But the most conspicuous item is the one I was hoping to find—a red wig. It's as bright as the crimson of my murder binder. Or the pool of blood around Morrie's body. Which means Tim may have been right. Vickie could have been a redhead doing Vegas.

And maybe doing Louie, too.

Sitting on the closet floor, I try to think of a way to nail down this supposition. Then it occurs to me: credit card bills. All of the records I searched through before were of cards in Morrie's name, but I've never seen a woman who didn't have a raft of cards in her purse.

On a top shelf, I spot some shoe boxes. Just the right size for keeping old checks, bills, or credit card statements. Each of the five boxes has the year noted on the end and side with a black marker.

I pull down the box for the current year. She's kept the

records in neat order: correspondence; credit card statements for an American Express card and a VISA card, both in her name; and monthly statements for the tennis club she belongs to. I glance through the correspondence, noting that it's mostly personal.

Now leafing through credit card statements, I see she doesn't charge many things, which, I suppose, is a benefit of having a large checking account. I wouldn't know. My sometimes-patient creditors have to wait for about a month.

She seems to charge meals at nice restaurants with her American Express card, paying it off the next month. Her VISA card is used for big ticket items such as expensive clothes, jewelry, and travel. In fact, from clothing purchases on her VISA card, I see she did travel to Nicaragua with Morrie on the second trip in June.

Ah, a fascinating discovery: the day Morrie took the first trip to Nicaragua last November, Vickie booked a flight to Las Vegas. So I retrieve my murder binder from Morrie's desk to check another date. Just as I suspected, on the same day as Morrie's trip to the Cayman Islands, Vickie also flew to the glitzy playground of the West.

Man. I've been using the wrong information in programming my investigation. Similar to what scientists did when they sent the Mars orbiter crashing into the planet.

A drink would hit the spot. I head for the fridge and find a Diet Coke, amble into the sunroom, and flop onto a soft chair to figure this out. Big swig. Now I realize Vickie wasn't just trying her luck in Vegas. At least, not at games of chance. It was more of a sure thing.

But how did it all come about?

Pulling out my notepad, I write down a few key words, circle them, then put them in random order around a central position. I'm creating my own solar system of thoughts.

Trying to get to the epicenter of this strange galaxy I've stumbled across.

And I see a pattern. The words and circles I'm jotting are getting fainter all the time; my pen's running out of ink. I'm sure I have a backup in my binder. Nope. Maybe my jacket pocket. No. Did Sir Isaac Newton or Albert Einstein ever have such plebeian problems?

There's a drawer in the small table beside my chair. Sure enough, there are a couple of pens in there. And a half-empty pack of cigarettes.

Marlboros. Extra longs. Same kind I found outside the fence.

What the hell does this mean?

I bundle the copied files, including Vickie's credit card records, to take home with me. Before leaving her house, I locate her passport and verify she didn't go with Morrie to Switzerland or the Caymans. And that she did go with him to Nicaragua in June.

Once home, I contemplate Vickie's trips to Vegas.

Binga seems to know I'm distracted. Even as I set down her food bowl, she looks at me oddly, cocks her head, and gives me a high-pitched whine. But it's difficult to explain artifice to a dog.

I'm restless all night. Binga sleeps with the peace of the dead, her sawmill-like snoring breaking up the few short periods during the night when I catch a few winks. I awake needing two aspirin and a strong squirt of eye drops. Milk and a bagel also help. Then it's back to my Expedition for another sally to the airport. Destination: L.A.

There's only one person I want to talk to here in La-La Land: Spots McElroy. Well, I might consider an intimate lunch with Demi Moore. Or Gwyneth Paltrow. But with regard to this case, Spots is my main man. At least, I hope he is.

The buxom receptionist gets more folding green down her front. I slip into the studio. Spots has lit up a brunette with a bigger chest than Hollywood Hulk Hogan. She might go far in this town. If she "makes" the right contacts.

When the scene's over, the director calls for a break and a change of scenery, which consists of putting a different-colored sheet on the bed and replacing the backdrop of a beach scene with one of mountains. Spots studies his lighting setup for a minute, shrugs, then shuffles toward the break room. I fall in step with him.

"You again?" he inquires. "Ain't you solved that case, yet?"

"I'm not on TV or in the movies. Takes me longer than an hour."

He frowns, drops some quarters into the machine, and hits the button for a Dr Pepper. He grabs the can, pops the top, and flops down at a scarred table. "Be a fine time for a cigarette," he says.

Patting my jacket pockets, I say, "Sorry, fresh out."

He sighs. "Hell, you don't smoke. And me neither. Some quack doctor just told me I was a year away from gettin' emphysema."

"You've got to listen to those guys, Spots. Sometimes they know whereof they speak."

"Maybe. But could be it's better to live three or four years happy than five or six miserable, you know what I mean?"

"Can't argue with that logic. Everything's relative."

"Maybe I should take up cigars like all the bimbos in this town."

"You know a lot of them, don't you?"

He chugs some Dr Pepper. I see visions of sugar dolls dancing in his lurid mind's eye. "Quite a few," he says. "I run across a lot of 'em right here. They'll do anything to get ahead in this dreamland."

I place the photo of Morrie and Vickie on the table.

"You said this woman looked familiar. She's a blonde here, but if you think of her as a redhead, would that bring back any memories?"

He picks up the photo, looks it over, and twists his mouth, thinking. "She looks familiar, but I can't recall any more than that."

I tap my red murder binder, trying to think of something to jostle his misfiring neurons. I'm pretty sure my hunch is right, but unless Spots can confirm it, I'm still just spinning a theory. In the investigative field, those are as worthless as fake moon rocks.

Two girls from the last scene sidle into the room, laughing, blowing smoke at the ceiling. They buy some sodas, their flimsy robes not concealing their obvious curves, and I note Spots taking it in. Funny, after all he's seen, he's still interested in . . .

Of course. Spots doesn't get many Garbos or Hepburns or Stones around here. He's not focused on faces, he's a T & A man.

I open the binder and scrabble through the photos encased in the clear plastic sheets. I'm looking at shots I took of the crime scene at Vickie's pool. And here's the picture I'm seeking.

It's one I took of the fence and the gray thread; Vickie stood to the side, but was still in the frame. It's a full body shot of her in her itsy bitsy bikini, with her cover-up open. Tight focus.

I toss it on the table. Spots gives one last look at the girls, then turns to look at the shot. His eyes open wider, then he starts to tap the back of the photo against a thumbnail, squinting in concentration.

"She could've been a redhead," I prompt. "Maybe bright red."

He smiles. "Son of a bitch. You're right, son. I remember her."

"You do?" Now I'm not so sure. Maybe I coerced him.

"You bet. Bright red hair. And look at those sculpted bazookas. I never forget a great pair of—"

"But is the face right, too? Or do you recall it?"

He snorts, then says, "Faces change with the eye shadow, lipstick, you know, all that shit women plaster on themselves. But a great set of—"

"So you're saying you remember her? She used to work here?"

"She was here for a few years. Flaming red hair, like you said. Up top, anyways. In fact, she was billed as Rhonda 'Red Rider' Jones. They called her that as a joke from the old cowboy hero."

"I get the reference."

"Sure you do. Yeah," he cackles, "she got that name doing a scene where she humped this actor was supposed to be a Texan?"

"Uh huh."

"And she was on top, sort of like being in the saddle, riding a buckin' bronco, or some such."

"Uh huh."

"And she had a line about how she heard Texans were supposed to have longhorns, you see, a double meaning joke?"

"I see."

162

"Then she forgot her next line, which was something dumb like: 'So poke me, cowpoke,' and she made up a line that went: 'So gore me, you big stud.' The line was a hit, the movie did good, and she even got fan mail."

"Wow, just like a Hollywood starlet."

"Right. So from then on we billed her as 'Red Rider,' and she was always on top of the guy. Sometimes she'd even wear a ten-gallon hat. Sort of a trade gimmick, you might say."

"Quite an image. Thanks for sharing."

"I sorta thought she might get some parts in legit films. She could act pretty good. But far as I know, she didn't."

"Do you know if she went out with Louie Minnelli?" I ask.

"He hit on every quiff around here, but I don't recall about her."

I start to say something, but he's staring at the wall, thinking, then he says, "I wonder whatever happened to her?"

"I'll bet she married some rich guy and lived happily ever after."

"Yep, I suppose it happens." He swigs his Dr Pepper.

"Truth can be stranger than fiction," I say.

He laughs. "Not when you're talkin' about the scenes they write around here. Sometimes the actors pull a muscle trying to follow the script."

Tough life. But now I think I know the actors in my drama. And they're going to get full screen credit for their parts.

Chapter 16

On the flight to Kansas City, I mull over the case. Could I be reading too much into the liaison between Vickie and Louie? Maybe they met at Sleek Enterprises years ago, then recently reunited, at least when Morrie was out of town. But that doesn't necessarily mean that one or both of them were involved in Morrie's death. Adultery is a lot more commonplace than murder.

Maybe more important is what Morrie's trips to the Cayman Islands, Switzerland, and Nicaragua mean in the scheme of things. Not to mention his laundering money for Sleek and Bahama Mama. And his connection with some shady underworld characters.

Kimberly said Louie took the rap for Morrie in the death of Kimberly's hooker friend, Tiffany. So was there some payback from Morrie to Louie? I stiffen in my seat. Of course, that's exactly the way the Mob operates.

They get Morrie in their debt, then ask "favors" from him which he can't refuse. He sets up accounts in Switzerland and the Caymans for laundering money for Sleek and Bahama Mama, probably both Mob fronts. It's payback for Louie's silence after Louie bought off Kimberly and then claimed he hit Tiffany, taking the heat for Morrie.

But why the trips to Nicaragua? Those don't seem to fit in with the other arrangements. Plus, Vickie went with him on one of them.

Besides, why would Morrie be bumped off by the Mob when he was doing exactly what they wanted? Which leads

164

me back in a circle as to whether Louie or Vickie might've killed him. Still, she'd already looked into divorcing him, so that doesn't quite fly, either.

I study my notes. Rhonda "Red Rider" Jones. Who would've thought Vickie had such a racy past? Like the flick about housewives being hookers.

Back to basics. Don't want to get confused by details which may be mere shooting stars—a little flash, but of no real meaning. Review the facts: Morrie was shot from a few feet away. Vickie shoots high into the trees at a "prowler." I find a shoe print, a cigarette butt, and a thread.

It's about time to call the FBI lab about the heel print, to see if they've identified the shoe type. And I need to resolve whether the Marlboros in the drawer in Vickie's sunroom are connected with the butt I found. I'll call Bagley, too.

But that reminds me about the mike at the jail, apparently to overhear me talking to Vickie. And I remember being followed. Still, I can't see a reason for the cops to watch me; besides, Bagley wouldn't put in an illegal mike. Would he?

I leaf through the murder binder, getting more confused. Just as physicists use a superstring theory to explain the interconnection and interaction among gravity, electromagnetism, light, space, and time to understand the workings of our universe, I must find a design that'll account for all the devious moves in this case. Ah, yes. Piece of cake.

When I land in Kansas City I call Bagley.

"How do you always know when I'm headed out the door?"

"Just helping you get overtime pay. Don't bother to thank me."

"In the interest of not breaking the Department's budget

and of me getting to my poker game on time, let's keep it brief."

"You got it. Just two things. First, did you hear anything from the FBI lab about the shoe print?"

"The report just came in. I called, but you were out. Where you been?"

"You don't want to know. What did the report say?"

"Expensive Italian shoe: Ferragamo. From the picture they sent, I wouldn't take 'em over a good pair of Lucchese boots, but they're supposed to be hot shit."

"I need to see the picture."

"I'll leave a copy with the receptionist at the desk. What else?"

"I'm thinking maybe we should try to get a DNA test on the cigarette butt. There may be enough saliva on it to bring it up."

"To compare with who?"

"I don't want to say now, but I have some irons in the fire."

"I bet they'll still be there when the fire is cold and dead."

"That's possible, Jeff, but humor me."

"If I can go grab a bite and get to my poker game, it's a deal."

"May you have handfuls of aces."

Back in Hillsboro I drive to the PD and pick up the picture of the Ferragamo shoes. I agree with Bagley, they're nothing I would wear even if I could afford them. But if memory serves, they sure look like what Louie was sporting when I confronted him in the casino.

Now my mind's whirling as I take Kansas Avenue south through town to 37th Street, turn past White Lakes Mall, then zip down Burlingame Road. Traffic is sparse, with darkness setting in. But even with my tough day I feel electrified; it could be I'm zeroing in on a good theory concerning this murder.

As my headlights hit my gravel driveway, I watch for Binga to come bounding out to meet me. Or at least padding out. But she does neither.

I check the front porch where she likes to lie, but see no big ears sticking up like furry antennae. The lights I left on in the kitchen and living room are still aglow. A light gleams upstairs, which I don't recall leaving on.

Sliding down my car window, I listen and watch. The doors and windows appear to be closed and intact. I see no movements, hear no noises in the house. Maybe I *did* leave the light on in my office.

It's quiet out here, except for the droning buzz of a far-off plane. A dog barks in the distance, but it's not Binga. Where the hell is she?

"Binga!" I yell. "Binga, come here!" Then I whistle. Nothing.

Now I'm worried. She's not the type to go out in the road and get hit by a car. But she is pretty old, which concerns me.

I climb out, headed for the back door, key in hand, when I hear a low groan. Startled, I pause and listen hard. It might be a wounded coyote, or even a cougar. We do get them out here on occasion.

There it is again. Beside the garage. Close to Binga's dog house.

I move over there. There's a dark shape lying on the ground. Binga lifts her head to look at me, then flops back to the concrete.

"Binga!" I go to my knees beside her, lifting her head,

trying to get her to look at me, to jump up and start prancing around and licking me. But she just lies there limply. "Oh, my God. What's the matter with you?" She groans again, then her eyes seem to roll up in her head, and she goes limp.

I rush to the truck, open the door, and return to Binga. I lift her in my arms like a heavy sack of flour. Her head hangs to one side.

My heart's pounding in my ears, and my chest tightens. Hobbling to the truck, I lay Binga on the floor, then jump in. I grab my cell phone and call John, my vet, who agrees to meet me at his animal hospital in fifteen minutes.

I roar away, with gravel spewing from my tires as I race into the night. On the tricky gravel road my Expedition slides to the side, giving me a sick feeling as the deep ditches reach for my wheels, but finally I reach the smooth blacktop, and I mash the pedal with a vengeance.

I'm listening as I drive, and I think I hear Binga breathing. Can't be sure, but . . . wait, there. She yips, as though she's dreaming.

"Hold on, girl," I say. "Just hang on. Dr. John will help you."

I zip past a truck, doing eighty, my heart thundering.

John's waiting for me, lights on, the doors to his exam rooms thrown open so I can carry Binga straight in and lay her on a stainless steel table.

"What happened to her?" John asks.

"I don't know. I came home and found her like this."

He places a stethoscope to her chest, then lifts her eyelids and peers at her pupils. He forces open her mouth; there's white froth.

"Rabies?" I ask. "Could she have been bitten by a rabid squirrel or skunk?" No, wait, she had her shots this summer. "Can she get rabies even if she's had her shots?"

John grabs my arm and points to a chair. "Take it easy, Max, I'll handle it. You sit down and try to relax. I don't need two patients."

I head for the chair, then turn, "But do you think it could be—"

"No, I'm pretty sure it's not rabies. Especially if she's had her shots. I imagine she's eaten something bad."

"You mean like rancid meat or something?"

He turns to a cabinet, searching inside. "I think she may have been poisoned. I'm going to try to bring her back before it takes her."

An hour later, Binga is sleeping soundly in a pen at the attached kennel. John and I are drinking sodas and chuckling at stupid jokes we've recently heard. I'm giddy and talking and laughing loudly.

John says, "So I'd better get over to my kid's school program. Don't worry, Binga will be all right. She just needs to sleep it off."

"No permanent effects, you think?"

"She should be fine. You must've come home soon after she ingested it. But you'd better check around the place and find out what she got into."

"I'll do it tonight," I say.

The drive home is lonely, as I contemplate sleeping by myself in my country house. First Sharon gone, now Binga almost lost. But, thank God, Binga should be okay. She'll go some day, but I'm not ready for it yet.

When I get home, I decide to check in the garage to see if she got into anything there. But the garage door is completely down, and the entry door is closed. So I switch on a flashlight and search the ground around the dog house.

There's a chewed bone lying on the concrete beside her house. It's from a T-bone steak. Still has some gristle and meat on it.

I sure didn't leave her any steaks to munch on while I was gone. I only eat half a dozen a year myself. So who fed her one, and why?

She could've wandered around the area and found the bone in someone's trash. But that wouldn't explain her getting so ill that John thought she'd eaten poison. Unless she got into something else.

Opening the door to my house and turning on the lights, I freeze. Now I'm pretty sure someone gave Binga a poisoned steak, because it looks as if a burglar's been here. The laundry room's a mess, with dog food, tools, and detergent pulled down from storage shelves and strewn across the floor.

The kitchen's torn up, too. The dishes and pots and pans have been set on counters. Stuff from the freezer left out to get soggy, while eggs and milk and pickles sit around like so much junk.

Why would anyone go through all that crap?

I take another look at the door, spotting some jimmy marks I missed earlier. So they wanted to disable Binga while they got into the house. But wait a minute. I stand still, listening, but hear nothing. Then I unlock the basement door, ease down a flight of wooden stairs, and search in the box where I keep my big .357 Magnum.

The revolver's still there. With shaky hands, I twirl the dial on the combination lock that's fastened over the frame. On the second try I open the lock, then shut the loaded cylinder.

It doesn't sound or feel like anyone else is here, but you never know. So I start my search. After ten minutes of looking through the torn up house, I'm relieved I've found no one, and that most of my stuff wasn't damaged, just dumped out and rifled through.

The files I copied at Vickie's house are missing. Big surprise. Still, even if someone wanted the documents, how could he be sure I was gone?

No way, unless he'd seen me at the airport. But that's a pretty chance occurrence, unless he'd been following me all along. Or maybe someone saw me on the airplane. Though I didn't recognize anyone on the flight, or in the LAX airport.

Some people did see me at Sleek Enterprises: Spots, the master of lighting; the buxom receptionist; and now that I think of it, one of my main suspects for foul play, Carmine Lorenzo, the *capo* of skin flicks. But does he have contacts in Hillsboro?

I get a hollow feeling and a shiver travels along my spine. I rub my arms, trying to shake it off. My cell phone jangles, and I jump.

"Hey, Max, it's Jim Barber." My FBI buddy. "I looked at those blueprints you gave me," he says, "and I'd like to discuss them with you. I'm leaving town tomorrow afternoon, so I could either do it tonight or in the morning."

Much as I hate to, I'd better talk with him tonight. I'm not going to sleep much, anyway, and I don't like looking at this mess. I make sure I have my car keys, then lock the door.

"I found something odd in those blueprints," Jim says.

Just what I need. We sit down at his dinette table. The set of blueprints from Morrie's cubby hole in the closet are all spread out.

Jim points at an item on the blueprint. "Know what this is?"

"Looks like a computer station to me."

"That's right, but look." He stabs the print in numerous places.

"There's a lot of them?" I say.

"Exactly. And check this out." He pulls out a drawing that's a type of schematic. "See toward the center of the complex here? That's a central operating system. The other stations are satellites. It's an integrated system for all the buildings in the complex."

"I've had a rough day, could you spell it out in block letters?"

He regards me for a moment, then says, "So if this is supposed to be an industrial park, it makes no sense to have everything connected like this, with one centralized operating system."

"I suppose I get that."

"There should be different businesses leasing the buildings, each with their own computer system, with no reason for them to be interconnected. You'd find this layout at a corporate headquarters, where everyone's doing business for the same company. They can access company files and memos, exchange E-mail, whatever."

"I think I follow you. So my galactic theory may be viable."

"How's that?" He crosses one long leg over the other, his size fourteen Reebok basketball shoe bouncing up and down.

"Think of this complex as our solar system. The central system is the sun, and the rest of the buildings are planets and moons revolving around it, connected by gravity. It all whirls together."

He jiggles his big boat faster. "I'm with you, to a point."

"And I have a suspicion that this complex may, like our

sun, be only part of a galaxy of stars. There might be a number of them across America. Hey, with the way crime gangs are running rampant in Russia and Asia, this might be part of an international operation."

I think Jim's taken aback. Besides, he can't do anything more to help at this point. So I wind it down, saying I'll work on it some more and contact him if any of my wild theory proves viable.

As I drive, I muse about the industrial park Morrie was going to build. Two sets of plans, one standard for this type of complex, and a later set that's configured much like a corporate headquarters. The latter blueprint being drawn about when Morrie may have become beholden to Louie and his crowd. Something is definitely afoot.

The Bahama Mama offices and the other buildings were arranged, much as moons or planets or satellites, around the center pavilion. All part of a system. Barber shop, grocery store, travel agency, all connected. And consider the auto repair shop—the one that doesn't take unknown customers—an elite shop that "repairs" only certain vehicles. Or perhaps they chop them up to sell as parts.

They seem to be various components of a central operation, much as the phalanx of buildings of which Sleek Enterprises in California was a part. Of course, that setup was once a movie studio lot. Still, I'll bet that the Mob, or whoever is behind this, may have updated their methods since those early operations were conceived.

If so, how many more of these "corporate" offices might there be around the country? If they're going to build one in Hillsboro, although it is a crossroads in the U.S., still it makes me wonder how many they're planning. And what is their purpose?

As I mull it over, it starts to make sense. Such a complex

Mark Bouton

here in the Midwest could be used as a way station to smuggle drugs from Mexico or Colombia to Chicago and Detroit. Or as a place to chop cars stolen in the area. Even as a spot to store hijacked cargo until it's fenced, or possibly to hide fugitives on the run.

Maybe organized crime, which the FBI thought it had trampled, has risen from the ashes of its old empire. In younger hands, it might become better organized and more efficient. Probably more profitable.

So if Morrie got in the way of their operations, they wouldn't hesitate to rub him out. Or maybe now they'd say delete him. Which, as I tread the brake for a stop sign, makes the hair stand up on my neck and arms. Because I've managed to make myself a big thorn in the paw of a brawny, vicious, and probably very angry lion.

I wonder what would have happened if I'd been home when the "burglar" came to call? Would I have been dealt with the way he handled Binga? And now that I have a moment to reflect on it, the effrontery of someone breaking into my home really eats at me.

The gall of them to poison Binga, just so they could burgle documents. Some people say they don't get mad, they just get even. But I'm pissed. And I'm going to do more than just get even.

174

Chapter 17

As I pull into my driveway, painfully aware of Binga's absence, I try to approach the crime scene as though I were the perp. I'm trying to see things through his eyes, attempting to analyze his thoughts. If I uncover his behavior and traits, maybe I can figure out his identity.

The house is set back a good ways from the road, and I don't think anyone would come this far onto my property to do a burglary without knowing I wasn't here. Maybe Carmine Lorenzo tipped them off that I was in L.A. today. Or maybe I was tailed.

Whoever it was must have known about Binga. People don't usually carry poisoned steaks in their cars. So that rules out anyone who's not local, unless they got help or advice from someone local.

All right, step by step. The guy drives up, knowing I'm not here. Binga comes out to challenge the car, and the guy (or gal) tosses out the steak. Binga folds, and the burglar forces his way into my house.

So I'll do a crime scene search, starting with the outside and working my way in. With my flashlight, I check out the driveway, but see no tire tracks and no beer cans, cigarette butts, or gum wrappers. But as I approach the house, the beam hits something so bizarre I can't believe it. Even though I'm angry, I break out laughing. Shit.

Binga is a great dog and a friend. But as she's aged, there's a habit of hers that's annoying. Her hips are arthritic, and she doesn't go far from the back door to do her doggy dump.

I've learned to watch the lay of the land from my Expedition to the porch to avoid stepping in a fresh pile. But a stranger to my place, who has other business in mind, might not be so observant. Indeed, one wasn't, because I see a squashed dropping in the grass.

As I examine it from close range, I can see a definite heel print. I open the back hatch of my Expedition and pull out my camera. A couple of flash shots should do it. Then I'll spritz it with hair spray or something, dig it up, and put it into a shoe box as evidence.

Entering the mud room, I spot no smelly footprints. The guy must have wiped his shoe in the grass. No matter, I already have one print preserved. Chuckling, I imagine the lab guys opening the box.

I search the floor, counter tops, mirrors—anyplace there might be a fiber, hair, fingerprint, or dropped item. In the bathroom there's a large mirror, and I examine it closely. But I see no prints.

Then I spot a second clue. On the vanity top by the sink there's a black hair. The guy had to stare at himself in the mirror and smooth his hair. Creep. I grab an envelope and slip the hair inside.

Checking the rooms, I see that my television, computer, and fax machine are here, stuff that a junkie or teenage burglar would quickly glom onto. I don't have jewelry and don't keep cash in the house. The guy apparently grabbed the records, looked for any more, then split.

But I still have to check upstairs. Moving up the carpeted stairs, I realize how quiet it is here without Binga. And Sharon.

I'm starting to feel empty inside. I love my privacy, but maybe I need more contact with others. Especially someone significant.

I'd better get this done. I know I won't sleep well until Binga has recovered and I've identified this asshole. Then maybe I can put him away among big, gross guys who'll gladly pat his hair into place.

I find nothing more. There may be fingerprints on some of the pieces of paper scattered here and there. But aside from that . . . I glance around my bedroom . . . there's nothing else I—

But maybe there is. I lie down on my bed, snuggling into the pillow. Then I turn my head to look at the picture of Sharon on my end table. Just as I thought, it's out of place. Someone picked it up.

Using a handkerchief, I lift the frame. And as the overhead light glances across the glass, which I cleaned a couple of days ago, I spot a clear thumbprint. Gotcha, you prick.

I take the glass out of the frame and put it into a paper bag. Then I sigh, realizing how tired I am. I'll call the sheriff's office in the morning, but for now, I need to get some sleep, perchance to dream about who or what I'm up against.

Waking from a restless night, I glance toward Sharon's picture, but find it lying flat on the end table. Then I recall. Quickly, I call the veterinarian. He says Binga's doing fine, but he wants to watch her for another day, just to be sure.

As I toast a bagel, I decide how I'll handle the burglary. Perhaps I won't call the sheriff. When wrongs are this personal, the only satisfying way to set them straight is with in-your-face revenge.

I call Detective Bagley and tell him I need a favor. I want to compare the fingerprint on the picture glass frame to the set of prints Phil Emerson sent me from Vegas. The prints of my old nemesis, Louie Minnelli. I'll give odds right now they'll match.

Next, I carry a cup of coffee outside to examine the partial heel print in the doggie doo. In the light of day, it looks gross. But still, the birds sing and the squirrels gather acorns for winter. Human events seem of little consequence in nature's larger scheme.

I've brought out my red murder binder, and I leaf through it, finding the page with a copy of the footprint I found outside Vickie's fence. I hunker down to check the two patterns. Damn, they look identical to me. I'll be careful digging up the poop in case it might be used as hard evidence. But for now, this is all I need to convict and sentence Louie Minnelli in my personal court of justice.

No one screws with my dog, my house, and my wife's picture.

I sit on my porch swing, trying to think calmly. The pasture grass sways in the morning breeze, a tapestry of orange, yellow, red, tan, and gold. I'll try to weave the solutions to my problems together that cleverly, exacting revenge on Louie and also solving this case.

I dress and hit the road, stopping at the animal hospital long enough to pet Binga's head and say hello. A few minutes later I pull into the police parking lot. Bagley's in, chugging his own huge mug of java. He doesn't look that happy to see me, but then, he's never in that great a mood: he's a detective.

"You hear we nailed the turd who killed the preacher?" he says.

"Yep, I heard it on the news. Terrific. You're not getting older—"

"Yeah, yeah," he says, waving a hand in dismissal. "You wouldn't be layin' it on so thick unless you wanted something."

"One o'clock today. You and me and two big sirloins at

The Timberline. Never say I don't appreciate dedicated public servants."

"You're on, big spender. I knew I shoulda gone with the feds."

"Aw, the way they shower you with money there's too many decisions to make: tax shelters, mutual funds, IRAs. It's stressful."

"I should have such problems. So what do you want now?"

I tell him about my break-in, the footprint in the dog dung, and the fingerprint on the glass. He reluctantly takes the glass and the shoe box with the smelly evidence. "I'll give it to Franklin in Ident."

"I'll bet he'll have it ready in about . . ."

He rubs his forehead and closes his eyes. "Shit. Let's go do it now. Then maybe you'll leave and I can get some other work done."

"You're a devoted and accommodating detective."

"I'm just devoted to putting in another two years so I can dump this job. Let's go." And he pushes his bulk up from the desk.

I study him a moment, wondering if he might have put that bug in the jail's interview room.

He shrugs into his jacket, tightens his tie, and picks up the evidence. "What're you staring at?" he says.

"I think I saw Jay Leno wearing that same tie on TV last week."

"Sure, and I gotta shine up my Ferrari after my shift."

Harry Franklin is short, round, and thin on top. Still, he's one of the most cheerful guys around the PD. And a topnotch lab man.

"Hey, fellas, what you got for me today?"

"Max asked me who was our expert on hi-tech lab work, and I told him it had to be you. I figure you're the only guy knows how to handle sensitive evidence like this."

Harry eyes the shoe box suspiciously. Then he looks at me, and I shrug. "So let me have it," he says.

I'm afraid Bagley won't be able to resist, but he slides the box across the counter and stands there, hands on hips, saying nothing.

Harry hefts the box, thankfully not shaking it. He lifts a corner of the top. He can't see inside well, so he pulls off the lid.

"Holy shit," he says, turning his head away.

"We may be blessed with a good clue," Bagley says, howling at Harry's distress, "but I wouldn't say it's achieved sainthood."

Harry fumbles the top back on, but the aroma lingers. Maybe I should've spritzed it with more hair spray.

"We've got photos of a footprint at the murder scene of that developer, Morrie Jacobsen. Compare 'em ASAP, and give me a call. Then I got one more thing."

Now Harry doesn't look quite so cheerful. "You've about used up your favor coupons, pal."

"Now, Harry, come on. That fluffy-assed cat of yours craps, too. Don't be so high and mighty."

"But not where folks step in it. And she covers it up."

"I'm sure she's well-trained. Listen, I need a rush job, like five minutes ago, on the print on this piece of glass. Here's a set of arrest prints I want you to check it against. It looks like a thumbprint."

"I know it looks like a thumbprint, you moron. I look at fuckin' fingerprints all day." He shakes his head as he carries the glass to a work table, sprays it with a blue fluorescent powder, then shines an ultraviolet light across it. He scans the print for a moment with a round fingerprint magnifier, then looks at Minnelli's arrest prints.

He's shaking his head, and I get a cold feeling in my gut.

Now he raises up. "Nope. Definitely no match."

Bagley turns and looks at me.

My mouth feels dry. "Are you sure, Harry?"

He studies the prints again, although I can tell he's just going through the motions. Harry doesn't make mistakes in the lab.

Straightening up again, he shrugs. "Sorry. No match."

"Thanks for checking," I manage to stammer.

"Let me know what happens with the laser feces comparison," Bagley says, barely able to keep a straight face.

"Laser this, asshole," Harry says, turning around, bending over and lifting the tail of his lab coat. "And don't forget. Your chits have been called in for a long time in this office."

Bagley waves as though shooing a fly away. "Don't be such a hard ass, Harry. It's just another crappy day on the job. Try to remember to stop and smell the roses."

We leave Harry spewing a string of curses that I'm surprised he even knows. We all have our limits. Truth be told, I'm close to mine.

"Sorry about the fingerprint," Bagley says. "You thought this Minnelli was good for the burglary?"

"I had a strong feeling on it."

"Who the hell is he, anyway?"

I study his face. He's not being coy, just asking with a cop's curiosity. So I realize he didn't plant the bug because Vickie and I discussed Minnelli.

"You all right?" he says. "You look spaced out."

"Let's find a private room. I need to tell you something."

181

"Can't talk about it in the squad room?" he says, frowning.

"Sometimes the walls have ears."

We stop in an empty office. In ten minutes I brief Bagley on what I've been doing and who I think may be involved in this matter.

"Jesus," he says, "you're going up against some heavy hitters."

"I've got you and some good agents on my side."

"We're not with you all the time, and those guys don't fool around."

"I know," I say. "That's why I'm going to destroy their world."

He hitches his shoulders and adjusts his holster. "What can I do to help?" Jack's a good man to have on your side in an alley fight.

"I'm going to ask you another favor. You probably won't like it."

"If it's legal and will help you, don't worry about my delicate sensibilities. Shoot."

"First, let me tell you more of what I've found." I fill him in on being tailed, threatened, and, lastly, being bugged at the jail.

"Damn it, Max. You're turning *my* day into a piece of crap."

"I know. I'm sorry. But it's all just speculation, and I could, like the shoe box we gave Harry, be totally full of shit."

"How can we check it out?"

"Remember before Vickie's hearing you called and asked if I had more information in the case?"

He purses his lips. "Yeah, sure."

"Why did you do that?"

182

"I think I was just checking."

"But you knew I'd turn over anything I had."

"Yeah, I knew that. We were talking about the case, and it came up that maybe we should get back with you before the hearing."

"How'd it come up, Jeff?"

He studies his knuckles a few moments, thinking. "It was just a bull session in the squad room, and . . ." His face relaxes. "I remember, Bill Wahr said it."

"Okay, then here's the favor I need. Go back to Harry and have him check the print on the piece of glass against Wahr's prints."

"God damn it, Max. This sucks."

"Sorry." Then I remember there were two guys in one of the cars I thought was shadowing me. "Could you also check his partner's prints?"

Chapter 18

At the animal hospital, the vet's assistant, a plump, pleasant girl in her twenties, tells me Binga is doing well enough to go home. When the old gal gets released from her cage, she seems elated, her tail wagging like a metronome. I think I even detect a smile.

Sailing along Wanamaker, I take in the spectacular fall foliage. A light morning breeze tinkles through a tall, backlit, gold and green cottonwood. Elms glow yellow-gold, sumacs shine hot scarlet, and pear trees gleam in vivid hues of purple and lemon.

Turning up the radio, I find Radio Rich and Louann hosting 94 Country. She's a sweetheart, and he's the wittiest guy on radio. I laugh at his jokes and sing along with some of the songs.

Binga seems happy just sticking her snout out the window to suck in fresh air. I suppose the atmosphere she's been in lately is much like the shoe box I left at the lab with Harry Franklin. Pungent.

Which reminds me of the thumbprint on the glass that wasn't Minnelli's. And makes me wonder if Minnelli really *is* involved in this matter. My cell phone warbles, and I answer it.

"Hey, Max, it's Jeff Bagley. I got some bad news."

Sounds like another miss on the fingerprint. "What's that?"

"I'm afraid you were right. The thumbprint on the glass was Bill Wahr's. I can't believe it."

All right! "I'm sorry about that. But at least now we know."

"I don't feel like I know much of anything at this point. Why would one of our detectives steal your records and poison your dog?"

"I don't know, I'll have to give it some thought, Jeff."

After a pause, Bagley says, "Harry did a comparison on the stinky heel print, too."

"What'd he sniff out on that?"

"Max, you'd joke about your own funeral. Okay, that was a match to the heel print you found at the Jacobsen crime scene."

So maybe Minnelli *is* in the picture. "That's good, Jeff."

"Do we know who the shoe fits?"

"Someone who left the ball early."

"Christ. And there's something I didn't tell you before. Wahr and his partner have had problems before. They're teetering on the edge of getting fired."

"Would it have anything to do with missing funds?"

"Damn. How'd you know that?"

One of the oldest incentives in the books. "Just a guess." And a real good reason why they might be helping a lucrative operation like the Mob. "You got probable cause to check their financial records?"

"Consider it done."

"Sorry for the bad news, Jeff."

"Hell, I'm just glad to know it now. Nothing worse than a dirty cop."

"I know." Except maybe a dirty mobster.

"Oh, I just heard Vickie Jacobsen got out on bail an hour ago."

"Good. And tell Harry thanks for his help."

"Nah, he don't feel right unless he thinks he's performing a thankless job. Gives him more reason to bitch all the time."

"I thought he was a pretty cheerful guy."

"He is. Bitchin' is what makes him happy."

"Gotcha. Bye."

Binga eyes me questioningly.

"I'm going to put these guys away, girl. You don't have to worry. It'll just take a little time." And some good ideas.

Once home, Binga sniffs around the yard, then does another number two close to the back door, possibly laying another trap for a bad guy. Meanwhile, I have a revelatory thought, like when Newton got conked by the apple.

I toss Binga her evening biscuit. Once she settles in on her mat, I sit down at the dining room table to flip through my murder binder. Ah, there's an invoice with the logo for The Lugio Brothers. It shows the office phone number in Detroit. Let's find out if they're part of this crooked cosmos.

Just as a solar eruption causes charged particles to glow at the north pole, producing the aurora borealis, I'll send a flare into the Mob world, or what is probably a satellite of the outfit, to see what lights up. I'm hoping it'll set off sparks, illuminating Louie Minnelli like the Northern Lights. Glow, little glowworm.

I punch in a number, a flat female voice says, "Lugio Construction."

"Put on Reggie," I say. "Tell him it's a close personal friend."

"What's your name?"

"Just tell him it's Louie."

The phone goes quiet, then, "Hey, is this Long Dong Louie?"

"Not even BB Balls Minnelli. But we're close." Like light years.

"You better be, using his name to get me on the phone. Who the hell is this?"

"My name's Max Austin, in Hillsboro."

"Where?"

"It's a small Midwestern town. Morrie Jacobsen used to live here. Before he passed on unexpectedly."

A moment of silence. "Okay, wiseass, who the hell are you?"

"I'm the guy who's going to clue in the feds about your operation unless you meet my demands."

"This some kinda joke? 'Cause I'm not laughing. And I might just send some guys to fuck you up, you get smart with me."

"Now, Reggie, you shouldn't make terroristic threats in a long distance call that might be recorded." Why didn't I think of that? "The feebs really hate that, you know."

"Hey, quit screwing around. What you want?"

"I know about the complex Morrie was going to build here. The same setup you have in Miami, Los Angeles, and other cities."

"The fuck you talkin' about?"

"And I know Minnelli is a wheel in setting it up."

"You doing a lot of talkin', but you ain't saying nothing."

"I don't have to talk about this any more. And I'll never get in your face again, either. For the right price."

"Assuming I had any idea what you're yakking about, and any interest in you, what's your price?"

"Two million dollars. Small, used bills. Delivered by UPS to my house by tomorrow."

"Uh . . . where's that?"

"Ask Long Dong." I hang up, noticing my hand is sweaty.

★ ★ ★ ★ ★

I check my locks and hide some guns and knives within quick reach. That accomplished, I start the oven to bake a couple of Cornish hens. When they're done, Binga eats hers heartily, but I only pick at mine.

Then I call Vickie, asking if I can come over tomorrow morning.

"That'll be fine, if it doesn't take long," she says.

I tell her it won't. I say it'll probably be late morning, since I need to catch up on some sleep. Ha.

After tossing about all night, waking whenever the coyotes get louder than usual, or I hear a bump, or creak, or moan of the wind, I find I'm exhausted but unable to lie in bed anymore by seven o'clock.

Rolling out, I rouse Binga, who looks good, and we limp outside. A breeze blows cool and refreshing, the leaves dancing to its melody, the birds singing its praises. Sunlight spills across the yard and onto my porch.

If a sniper hits me, at least I'll go happy. But I glance around to cut the odds, mainly because of Binga. And for a moment I feel sad that there's no one else for me to look out for or who cares for me.

My cell phone sounds off inside. I hustle back to the kitchen and snatch it off the counter, surprised to hear Amy Harrington.

"You haven't called me," she says, "so I'm being a brazen hussy and phoning you. Besides, I've been worried about you. And I'm wondering what's going on in your investigation."

So someone does care. "I've been lying low, trying to assess what I might've uncovered so far."

"Have you heard Vickie's out?"

"I have. How's she doing?"

"She's cooler than I'd be in her place. She wasn't thrilled being in the slam. But for some reason, now she doesn't seem too worried about getting convicted."

"You think she will?"

"Tell me something to make me think otherwise."

I ponder that a moment. Lawyers don't make very good confidantes. They're too used to talking.

"You're holding something back, aren't you?" she accuses.

"I doubt that it's jelled enough to make sense to you yet. Give me another day or so." Or maybe a lifetime.

She sighs. "Just keep me apprised of what you've got."

"You'll be the first to know."

"But don't overdo it, we've got two months until trial."

"Piece of cake, Amy. I'll call you soon."

"Seems I've heard that one before. But a girl can always hope."

For a moment, I'm tongue-tied.

"Max?"

"Sorry, I thought I had to sneeze, but it passed."

"You have allergies?"

"Only to murderers, but I'm about to vaporize one."

Binga bumped into something while I was in the shower, and I jumped an inch off the floor, which is high for me these days. Guess I must be on edge. After all, I just tugged on supermobster's cape.

As I dress, I'm thinking I'd better play things safe. I double check my .357 Magnum revolver, then load it with copper-jacketed hollow points. Cinching my belt is tricky, as I pick out a special one with a two-inch blade in the buckle. I snap a cartridge case with extra ammo on my belt and slip a pair of brass knucks in my back pocket.

For the *pièce de résistance,* I pin a large safety pin into the top inside part of my coat jacket in the back. Perfect for holding a flat, double-edged throwing knife. I can feign scratching the back of my neck and hit a man at ten feet in a split second. At least, I can hit a target that resembles a man. Or could when I was in practice.

I call Vickie to say I'm on my way. Another fine day greets me: sunny, mid-fifties, with a south breeze. But I know the winds will soon shift to the north, bringing colder, less hospitable climes.

Binga's inside, where I hope she'll be safe. I assume whoever burgled me got everything they wanted and won't be back. I hate to leave, but I have to resolve this case.

And because of the attack on Binga, I feel a red hot desire for revenge. But I don't want my anger to bring me down to the crooks' level. Tacky behavior is not my style.

I've found that it's best to stay cool and observe what's going on if you want to stay in control of a situation. And, as I whiz along Wanamaker, I spot a Chevy parked on a side road. When I pass by, it starts to move. Pulls onto the road behind me, trails at a distance.

I pass some milo fields, the stalks heavy with russet heads; corn fields, withered and dead; and acres of soybeans, their yellow leaves like hammered gold disks. A season for all things. And in my mirror, I see that the Chevy's still in season.

Of course, Wanamaker is a main road north into town. So, just for argument's sake, I turn right on 77th Street, sail along it at a good clip, then slow as I approach a stop sign at Burlingame Road. Check the old rear view mirror. Here comes the Chevy.

So I bend a left onto Burlingame. The Chevy hangs

back, not trying to catch me, content to follow. I think it's time to shake it.

Stopping at 61st, I wait until some cars near, then floor it, shooting across the intersection, squealing into a left turn. The Chevy will have to wait for the cross traffic. I build up a lead.

Back at Wanamaker, I turn right and roll past Washburn Rural High, where band members are practicing in the grassy field west of the main building. The Chevy's barely visible in my rear view mirror.

I speed toward a four-way stop. Good timing. I get to the intersection just before cars coming from either side slow. I roll through the stop sign and stomp the pedal, gaining distance.

There's a guy who lives just past Jay Shideler School, on the left behind a growth of trees. His driveway is out of sight. If my tail doesn't see me make the turn, he'll think I went over the next hill.

I'm far enough ahead that it should work. If no oncoming traffic slows me down. Almost there, and no one's approaching.

Except that a huge lime green garbage truck suddenly lurches forward to the next trash cans. It looks three stories tall. Guess I'll whiz on by. No, I can make it. I hit my signal, hoping to slow down the truck driver. I can make the turn if he'll just . . .

I hit my brakes and whip the wheel to the left, skidding. The other driver stands on his brakes, the grinding behemoth shuddering. It slows enough that I slide by with a foot to spare.

Now I angle the wheel back to the right, clip the branches of a cedar tree, and roll behind the heavy growth of bushes and trees. I'm invisible from the street. Trembling, I thank the lord of trash truck drivers for giving the man good reflexes.

I proceed along the driveway until it circles past my friend's house. No one home, it seems. So I pull back out the driveway to within thirty feet of the road, stop, and wait. No one turns in, and I hear no sound of cars speeding by trying to catch another vehicle.

Wheeling out onto Wanamaker, I don't spot the Chevy, but still take a detour into the back part of Lake Sherwood subdivision. I wind around, then come out onto 37th Street, through the Wanamaker intersection, making a right on Belle Street, up the hill to Vickie's.

No one turns after me, and I pull into her driveway in one piece. Just another fun day in the life of a supersleuth. It's always a rush.

Vickie opens the door wearing cream slacks with a gorgeous cranberry blouse dripping in gold chains. Not your average housewife.

"Hi, Max, I was wondering when you'd get here."

"Sorry, I had traffic problems."

"No matter. I glanced into Morrie's office, and everything seems in place. But I thought you'd already copied everything."

I describe my burglary. She seems shocked. "Do you think someone might try to break in here, too?"

"Mine was probably an isolated event. Don't worry about it."

She looks concerned. "When you leave, I'll arm the system."

"Good idea. I'll just copy a few documents, shouldn't take that long. And don't let me interrupt whatever you're—"

"I'm just going through some clothes in the bedroom."

"But I would like to talk to you for a minute."

She glances at her watch. "All right. Let's sit in the sunroom."

"Great," I say, uneasy about confronting her.

She sits on a flower print settee. Two metal chairs with light green cushions are at a glass top table, and I set one down a few feet from her. Close proximity is more effective for close questioning.

"You look worried, Max. Is everything all right?"

"I hope so, but I've run across some troubling things."

"What sort of things?" She crosses her legs, jiggles her foot.

"First, there's the insurance money," I say.

"We talked about that. I thought you understood the situation."

"I did, too, but at the time I didn't know about Morrie's trips."

"What trips do you mean?"

"The ones to Switzerland, the Cayman Islands, and Nicaragua."

She gives a small shrug, adjusts her watch band, then says, "He was a businessman. He took quite a few business trips."

"And you went with him on one of the trips to Nicaragua."

"No, I . . ." But she hesitates and regards me.

"You were saying?"

"Now I remember, I did go on one trip. Morrie wanted me to see the country. He thought it was exotic, in a primitive way. And I thought the scenery *was* gorgeous."

"As opposed to the gaudy glitter of Las Vegas?"

Her eyes now seem less like warm blue pools and more

like cool azure quartz. "What brought that up?"

"Your trips there when Morrie went to the Caymans and Switzerland. And during his first trip to Nicaragua."

"I told you I had friends in Vegas. I sometimes visit there."

"And you told me Louie Minnelli was just a businessman that Morrie dealt with. Not, say, a close friend of yours."

She looks stunned. But she regains her poise. "You know, I recalled after we talked that Morrie *did* introduce me to Mr. Minnelli one time when we visited Vegas. And I ran across him when I was in one of the casinos by myself. But he's hardly what you'd call—"

"The casino at The Mirage?"

"Yes, I was there, forgetting that was where he worked. It was a big surprise when he saw me at the roulette wheel and said hello."

"May I ask, are you a big gambler?"

"I just get chips for a hundred. When it's gone, I call it a night."

"Then I don't see why the casino would comp you a room."

"They don't. I stay in a regular room like—"

"Not a suite, such as Louie Minnelli might have?"

"No, I told you—"

"There are no room charges on your credit card for those trips."

"Well, I . . ." She stands up, fidgeting with her hands. "This all means nothing, Max, and I do have some things to take care of."

"Sit down. I have a few more questions."

She stares at me, both angry and frightened. But she sinks down onto the settee. Her eyes resemble distant, cold blue stars.

"I found out you stayed with Minnelli in Vegas, but I'll cut to the chase. I also know about the flicks where you were 'Red Rider.' And I know you were hot with 'Long Dong' Louie in those days."

"How did you . . . ?" Then she closes her mouth.

I wait, sitting still and composed.

She gazes at her lap and turns her wedding ring around and around on her finger, her hands becoming blotchy.

Then she looks up at me. "All right. I'll tell you everything. Maybe I should have told you from the beginning, but, as you'll see, it really has no bearing on your investigation."

I can't wait to hear this.

Chapter 19

Vickie takes a deep breath and lets it out slowly. Then she looks into my eyes, searching. And even though she may not be lily white in this probable conspiracy, she still has the face of an angel.

"Just tell me all of it," I say. "No games. We're past that."

"You're right." Her eyes are aglow like a Siamese cat's. "I know you suspect the worst, but just let me explain. It all started when Morrie got in a bad scrape in Vegas."

I guess she means the murder of the hooker "scrape."

"So what happened?"

"Louie got Morrie out of a jam, which was great for us at the time, but then the Mob decided Morrie should pay them back."

"So Louie *is* connected."

She holds out a hand, palm up. "The Mob's not like you see in those *Godfather* movies. At least, the current group isn't. It's evolved into a business almost as legitimate as any other."

"How's that?"

"Okay, Max, you know about Enron, WorldCom, Arthur Andersen. But do you think Microsoft or Intel or Viacom are totally on the level? That is, ethically and morally?"

I think most businessmen are walking a thin line, but I'm not interested in a philosophical discussion. "Probably not. So?"

"They wanted Morrie to move money into overseas accounts."

"Launder it, you mean?"

"Whatever you want to call it. He'd receive checks, then transfer the funds to various accounts he set up in Switzerland and the Cayman Islands."

"And his associates could access the accounts?"

She shrugs. "There were numbered accounts in Switzerland, and Morrie set up a couple of international companies with several 'officers' who could write checks on the Cayman accounts."

"Would some of the checks have been from Sleek Enterprises?"

She blinks. "You *did* do your homework, didn't you?"

"I keep up with my lessons. Who else sent Morrie checks?"

She regards me a moment, then apparently decides I know anyway. "There was another business in Miami called Bahama Mama."

"Where'd they get the money that was being washed?"

"I don't know all the details. I think the money moved from Lugio Brothers to Minnelli Promotions, then to those other two companies."

"But that wasn't all they wanted Morrie to do, was it?"

She sighs and fidgets with her hands. But she looks resigned. "No, they wanted him to change the plans on his industrial complex. They were going to use it as one of their headquarters operations in the Midwest."

"Was Morrie going to do it?"

"Actually, he hated the idea. He didn't mind helping transfer funds, but he was afraid they might not pay him fully for the complex, which would bankrupt his business."

"So he decided to fight them?"

"Yes," she says, smoothing her slacks at the top of her

thighs. "We talked about it and came up with a plan."

"A plan to trick the Mob?"

"At least the ones like Louie and few others."

"How would it go down?"

She smiles, I assume at my police jargon. As they say, old habits die hard. Just like old supernovas, which go out with a hell of a bang.

"Morrie looked around and decided Nicaragua would be a good place for us to disappear. I took the trip there with him. As I said, it wasn't bad."

"Especially if you had a lot of money? Like, say, two million dollars from his insurance?"

"You don't miss much. It's too bad Amy called you to work this case."

"But how were you going to get it? With Morrie still alive, there'd have been no body."

"When I worked in California, I spent time at the beach. I knew several places where a car could go off a cliff and be crushed, probably burn, and for sure sink into the ocean where a body inside it would wash away."

"I don't get it."

"We were going to rent a car, send it off the cliff, and I'd tell the cops that Morrie had been in it."

"I'm not sure the insurance company would pay that amount unless a body was found."

"We thought of that, so we needed other funds, just in case."

Now a little light bulb goes on in my head. "The last checks from Sleek and Bahama Mama. Morrie didn't send them overseas."

"It amounted to slightly over a million dollars. That, together with the liquid assets we had, would have seen us through a lot of years in Nicaragua."

"So what went wrong? Why'd Morrie got whacked? Sorry, I mean murdered."

Now she squirms on the cushion, and I know I've gotten close to the central nerve of this fiasco.

"It goes back to Louie," she says, which doesn't surprise me.

"How's that?"

"As you said, we dated when I was making movies in California. At that time, I was pretty taken with him."

I guess it takes all types. I just nod and wait.

"Then Louie got sent to Chicago. I was tired of the porno stuff, and I realized it was never going to lead to anything in legitimate movies, so I decided to wipe the slate clean and move to Chicago, too. Luckily, I had my degree, so I had something to fall back on."

Besides her back? No, I guess she was on top.

"So you kept seeing Louie?"

"Yes, we got pretty close, even considered getting married, but then he had to go work in Vegas. I didn't want to go back there. I liked my life in Chicago. So I dragged my feet about leaving."

She sighs. Thinking about what might have been, I suppose. "Louie and I drifted apart. I met Morrie, we went out, and you know the rest."

"I know about your marriage, but I still don't know how Morrie ended up lying dead beside your pool."

Now her eyes glisten and a small tear trickles down her cheek; I guess she does have some feelings.

"Louie called for Morrie here a couple of times when Morrie wasn't home. We chatted, recalling old times. Then one time when Morrie had just left on a trip, Louie called, and he suggested I jet to Vegas and have a drink with him."

"So you did."

"I was curious. I hadn't seen Louie in five or six years."

"And wore a red wig?"

She looks bewildered. "You seem to know everything. It was as a disguise, and also because I knew Louie liked me as a redhead."

"I still don't know how Morrie died."

"It was accidental. Morrie held onto the Bahama Mama and Sleek checks. Then he cashed them, and we planned to fly to L.A. the next day."

"But what happened?"

"We were packing, when Morrie glanced out the back window and saw someone sitting in one of the chaise lounges by the pool."

"Who?" I have an idea, and it makes me feel clammy.

"It was Louie. Morrie went out there, and I followed. Louie was very angry. He confronted Morrie about the money."

"They knew it hadn't been deposited?"

"They were watching closer than we realized. Morrie tried to con Louie, but he wouldn't have it." She stares at her hands, shaking her head. "Twelve more hours, and we'd have been on the plane to L.A. with a million-and-a-half dollars in cash. Maybe more coming, if the insurance company paid the claim."

"How did it all go bad?"

"Before Morrie went outside, he stuck his revolver in the back of his pants. When Louie started talking tough, and threatened Morrie with the pole, Morrie pulled the gun, told him to drop it, and to get the hell out of there."

"What did Louie do?"

She wrings her hands and looks at me, her face pale and pleading.

"He dropped the pole, but he's a hothead, just like

Morrie was. It was like two rams bashing their heads together. Louie wouldn't leave. He told Morrie to put away the gun or he'd be sorry, and Morrie insisted he get out. They were both furious."

"So you got scared?"

She's nodding, tears streaming from both eyes. "I didn't want to see either of them harmed. But in that moment I realized Morrie had really hurt me by running around with other women, and that I had deeper feelings for Louie than I'd admitted to myself."

"What'd you do?"

"I picked up the pole and hit Morrie's wrist with it, knocking the gun loose. I wanted them to cool down before one of them got hurt."

"So what went wrong?"

Vickie stares at me as though I'm her father-confessor. Criminals sometimes make that mistake. But I can't give her penance. My purpose is to find the truth, and if it sets her free, that's fine. In most cases, it doesn't.

"What happened after Morrie lost the revolver?" I prod.

"They froze for a second, then both of them lunged for it."

"And you hit Morrie in the chest with the pole?"

Now she seems to deflate against the back cushion of the small sofa. "Yes, it was just a reaction. I didn't even think about it. But it knocked him back just long enough for Louie to scoop up the gun."

"And then Louie shot him?"

"No, no. It wasn't like that. Morrie was . . . enraged, both at Louie and at me, I suppose. He charged at Louie, they fought over the gun for a few seconds, then Louie managed to push Morrie backwards. He pointed the gun at Morrie and told him to chill out."

"But he didn't?"

"No, he was too angry. Morrie had a bad temper, but I'd only seen him lose control like that once before. I think he was frustrated from dealing with those Mob guys, and also because we were so close to getting away."

"What'd he do?"

"He grabbed the pole away from me and went after Louie. I think he would've killed him, but then Louie shot him. It was really self-defense."

I sit there in silence for several moments.

She's giving me a wide-eyed look of innocence, as if that's the end of a true confession, and I'm supposed to hug her like some talk show host.

"So why didn't you call the cops and tell them what really happened? Why did you tell that story about the prowler?"

"Louie was worried the cops would think he did it on purpose. He just didn't trust them. So he said I should tell them Morrie surprised a prowler."

"Then Louie went over the fence, and you fired a shot high over his head?"

She nods.

"But how did the shoe print and the cigarette butt get there?"

She blinks, then says, "Those things were just a coincidence. Some Peeping Tom must've been out by the fence the day before."

I look into her reddened, but even more vividly blue eyes, giving her a faint smile of understanding. Then I shake my head. "It won't fly, Vickie. The shoe print beside your fence matched one I found outside my house. And it's a brand of shoes I saw Louie wearing."

"But . . . I don't see what—"

I hold up my hand. "The cigarette was the same brand

as a half-pack I found in a drawer in your sunroom."

She starts to protest again, then her face goes hard, and I can visualize her as a tough dominatrix about to climb aboard a man. Red Rider, Red Rider, won't you come—

"He's not buying it," Vickie says in a too-loud voice.

Uh oh.

Chapter 20

"Nope," says a voice behind me. "He's too smart for his own good."

Without turning, I say, "Louie. What brings you to our fair city?"

I glance over my shoulder as he approaches with a .45 automatic that looks like a cannon. These guys are supposed to carry those little .22-caliber jobs. Doesn't he watch "The Sopranos?" Never saw *The Godfather*? He's dressed in black slacks and a black knit shirt, and sporting his infamous Ferragamos.

"I came to this bullshit town to find out what you knew. When you told Vickie you were coming to see her, it made it easy."

"You shouldn't have poisoned my dog."

"Whether I did or not, it don't make no difference."

"It does to me."

"Put your hands up and turn around."

I don't see any alternative, so I do. He pats me down, relieves me of my revolver and pulls the brass knucks from my pocket. This is going badly.

He sets my gun on the glass top table, several long feet away, and says, "Now sit down and shut up."

His social graces suck, but he's got the gun, so I sit. With nonchalance, I assess the distance between us. For now, it's too far.

"Can I ask another question?" I say. Hope he doesn't notice that I'm stalling for time to think and to distract him from shooting me on the spot.

Vickie gazes at him, and, thankfully, he has to look like a big man in her eyes, so he says, "Sure, I don't care how many questions you ask. Long as it don't take more than two minutes."

Short interview. "What about the fingerprints on the gun?"

Louie snorts, I assume in derision. "I wiped mine off, put Morrie's back on, then told Vickie to pick up the gun and shoot it."

"Fair enough," I say, having already figured that one out, then query, "Why weren't there any prints on the pole?"

He smirks. " 'Cause I wiped it down before tossing it in the bushes."

"And you guys had time to plant the footprint and the cigarette butt? The cops got there pretty fast."

Now Vickie speaks up. "Louie put the footprint there after he jumped over the fence. We figured they'd never match it to a pair of shoes in Vegas. And besides," she adds, giving him a hard look, "he was supposed to throw them away, just to make sure."

"Hey, these are four-hundred-dollar loafers."

"Anyway," she continues, "the police never found the footprint out there, and I couldn't very well point it out to them. Then, after they left, I thought of the cigarette bit. I lit it up, then tossed it outside the fence."

"But they never—"

"Hell, no. Even when the detectives came back and searched around some more, still no one saw it."

"So that when I found it, that helped confirm your little charade," I say, shaking my head.

"Yes, that was good," she says, "until you began digging into—"

"Hey, that's enough of this bullshit," Louie says. "Are you packed?" I assume he means Vickie.

She gets a pissy look. "I'm almost ready. He interrupted me."

Well, *excuse* me.

"And you got the dough?"

I assume he means the mil-and-a-half.

"Yes, it's in a duffel bag. Everything's in my bedroom. I'll be ready in five minutes."

But as she stands up to head for her bedroom, Louie gets a look on his face like a feral mongoose. "Don't bother, I'll get it."

She looks incredulous. "But I'm not finished packing. It'll just take a minute, then we can—"

"I'm really just interested in the cash," Louie says. "And I can get that myself." Then he grins in a menacing sort of way. "Together with the eight hundred large I skimmed from today's gross at the casino, that makes a chunk of change for me to party with."

Vickie's jaw goes slack. "Louie, I don't know what you're saying."

I clear my throat. "I think he's decided to go to the land of margaritas and sugarcane without you."

"What?" she says, hands clamped on her hips. Life can imitate the movies. Maureen O'Hara did the same thing when chewing out John Wayne.

Louie chuckles, which sounds like gravel in a cement mixer. "The bastard's right again. Yeah, you're a hot babe, but I got to thinking about those days in California when I could have any bimbo I wanted. And with this kind of bank-roll, things should be even better, you know? Sorry, honey."

"You're *sorry?*" Vickie shrills. "What do you mean, you're—"

"Excuse me," I say. "He means he doesn't need either of us in his future."

"What? This is ridiculous."

"He's on the money," Louie says, then glances at me. "You should have hit the tables in Vegas when you had a chance. You got good intuition."

Wow, he used a four-syllable word. He must've attended the organized crime post-doctorate program.

"When he kills both of us," I say to Vickie, "there'll be no witnesses, so no crime. At least nothing that they'll ever pin on him."

"But he can't do—"

"Yeah, I can," he says. Then he picks up my revolver from the glass top table. Damn, I could've used that.

"First I shoot you with this guy's gun. Then I shoot him with mine."

"But I don't see—"

"Shut up," Louie says. "If I should get stopped leaving this place, which I won't, I'll just say I came in here as this dickhead was shooting you, and I shot him."

"No one would believe that," she says.

And she's right, except that—

"But it's one of those cases, doll, of my word against my word. Corpses don't tell no tales."

Just as I'd reasoned.

"No, you can't do that, Louie." She sounds sad and plaintive, like a whistling arctic wind moving in the night. "We had plans."

But Louie must have run out of talking points. He's checking my revolver, and it won't be long before he—

No! As he points my gun at her lovely head, I feel a primal instinct to save her and to survive. Before I can reason it out, I step toward him, shoot a front kick into his knee, then grab at my belt.

The blade comes out faster and smoother than I could've hoped for. He's bent down now, grabbing his hurt knee, and I strike at the nearest target, which is his shoulder, thrusting the sharp blade deep into his flesh.

He screeches, very unlike a tough mobster, and drops my gun.

Then he turns toward me, his face splotchy, his eyes wide with pain and anger. Grabbing hold of the blade stuck in his shoulder, he yanks it free. In his eyes I see the ferocity of a wounded bear.

He lunges for me with the knife, and I backpedal, trying to get out of range, but my heel strikes a chair, and I feel myself falling, falling backwards, and see him coming over me, his hand raised with the blade held high, now striking down toward my chest—

When a loud bang buffets my ears, and he freezes in midair, his hateful gaze transforming into an icy stare, and his eyes losing their glint. Behind him stands Vickie with my revolver held in both trembling hands.

And Louie thuds to the floor beside me like an iron meteorite.

I kneel down and feel for a pulse at the carotid artery in Louie's neck. But there's no pumping going on. All kaput.

"Is he dead?" Vickie asks.

I nod. "It's all right, Vickie. You saved my life by shooting him. That's the same as self-defense."

"But what about Morrie's murder? Do you think I'll get out of that? Can I just say that Louie did it? Maybe that he threatened me to keep quiet about it?"

I stand up and glance down at the recently departed Louie, thinking it's a shame that no one in this room seems to give a damn about his death, then look back at Vickie. "I think that's one a jury will have to sort out."

She goes pale. "Max, I can't take that chance. Jail drives me crazy."

"I know, but I'm sure there'll be a trial."

"No, I'm going to Nicaragua, the way I planned."

"I can't let you go. You're under bond for murder. If I didn't stop you, I'd be aiding and abetting a fugitive."

"Max, we have over two million dollars in cash. Go with me. We'll have a great life together."

I'm stunned. But I'm also apprehensive. Vickie hasn't offered to hand over my gun, and it's making me nervous.

"That's a lot to think about after what just happened. And, you know, I feel sort of dizzy. Let's get some fresh air."

"But . . . well, all right, but we don't have much time."

I slide open the patio door, consider slamming it shut and running, but realize my stiff leg isn't up to it. So I look around, thinking hard.

"Let's sit at the table," I say.

We take a chair, shielded from the late morning sun by the canted umbrella, a breeze making little lapping sounds in the water behind me.

"Don't think too long and hard on this, Max. Go with your feelings. I know you're interested in me, I've seen it in your eyes." She lays my revolver on the table.

"You're a beautiful and intelligent woman. Okay, I'm tempted." Let's see, I'd live with a gorgeous gal in an exotic locale, with two big sackfuls of money. Not too bad a retirement plan. Beats the crap out of a 401K.

She taps her nails. "I have to finish packing. What do you say?"

"Could I take Binga, my German shepherd?"

She frowns. "I hate pets. They're smelly, dirty, and a lot of trouble."

Much like kids and the elderly. "What if I decide not to go?"

She sighs. "Just come with me. We'll be fine."

"I thought I was too old for you."

"You're a real man, I've seen that. And I need your support to get through this. So let's get moving, or we'll miss our flight."

I lean over and fiddle with the pole holding the umbrella, looking as though I'm thinking it over. "I'm sorry, it's a great offer, but I can't leave. My roots and my life are here in Hillsboro."

She picks up the gun. My hand freezes just above the button on the pole.

"Then I guess I'll have to travel alone. Let's go back inside."

"And what happens there?"

"I'm sorry, Max. I can't leave you as a witness."

Chapter 21

"But Vickie, if you get stopped before you get to Nicaragua, what's your story?"

She leans forward, the gun getting closer. "I'll tell the cops you found out Louie killed Morrie. Then I'll say Louie broke into my house, saying he came here to kill you."

"Then what?" Just a little nearer, please.

"He tied me up, but I got loose. Then I came in when he was about to shoot you. I picked up your gun and shot him, but he'd already fired."

"You sure have a lot of corpses to explain," I say. Then in a soft voice I add, "Hope you don't get your stories mixed up."

"What?" she says, leaning forward.

I push the button, the umbrella starts to drop, and her eyes get big. The umbrella crashes onto the table, and I can't see her, but I guess it didn't knock the gun from her hand, because there's a loud crack and a small hole appears in the umbrella. Another crack, and something whizzes by my head.

I duck and roll, and she fires another shot past me as I come to my feet. Grabbing a chair, I heave it at her, but she dodges. We circle the table. Then I break for the house, but she steps to the side of the umbrella and fires, hitting me in the arm. Damn, that hurts.

She coolly cocks the hammer.

First I fake to the side, then run toward her, lunging for the table. I shove it hard, screeching it across the deck, driving it into her, pushing her backwards toward the pool. She screams and tries to dig in her heels, but too late.

Crack! The shot zings over my head and hits the house. She sails off the deck and splashes into the glinting water; too bad it's the shallow end.

She comes up sputtering, but holding the gun. I pull a handkerchief from my pocket and clamp it to the gash in my arm. Then I limp over to poolside. "Let me help you out," I say.

She points the revolver at me and pulls the trigger. Click. Again, click. Now click, click, click.

"You only get unlimited shots in bad detective movies," I say. "Come on out, I'm sure the water's chilly."

She cocks back her arm. "Damn you!" she screams, then lets fly with my piece. It sails over my head, and, luckily, lands on the umbrella.

"Are you through?" I say.

She fingers wet hair out of her eyes. "All right, help me out."

I do. Then, ever the ingrate, she says, "This doesn't change anything. I can still claim that Louie killed Morrie, and that I did nothing wrong."

I pick up my revolver. It looks okay, so I stick it inside my pants. Gazing back at her dripping form I say, "How will you explain the money?"

She shrugs. "I found it in the attic this morning while looking for something else. And I didn't know Louie stole money from the casino."

"And all the bullet holes around here?"

She thinks about it. "You saw Louie out here and tried to shoot him, but you missed and he ran inside. You followed him, but he got the drop on you. Then you stabbed him, he tried to stab you back, and I picked up your gun and shot at him, but one of the shots accidentally winged you."

"And when I tell what really happened?"

"That'll be your word against mine. And my story is stronger than the wild-eyed version you're telling."

"I agree with you, except for one thing."

"What's that?" She picks up a towel from a chair and dries her face, then goes to work on her hair. Her clothes are stuck to her body, and for a moment I reflect on the good life with her at a beach in Nicaragua.

"Actually, it's my word and your word against you," I say, lifting my shirt to reveal the microphone taped to my chest.

"You son of a bitch."

"And I thought you liked me."

"No one likes you, Austin," says a voice from the sunroom.

Some days bad dialogue is pandemic.

Two men are standing at the patio door, dressed in cheap sport coats with wrinkled pants and bad ties. Lousy haircuts. One of them is Bill Wahr.

"Well, well, two of Hillsboro's finest detectives," I say. "More's the pity."

"Ditch the gun," says Wahr, pointing his Glock automatic in an unfriendly manner.

"Maybe you don't count well," I say. "It's empty."

"Lose it." He steps out onto the deck, his partner close behind.

No one trusts anyone anymore. I lay it gently on the deck, then straighten up. "There you go, Wahr. Now what'll we do?"

"Now we'll have to shoot you in self-defense."

This is getting tiresome. "You realize my recorder is still running?"

Wahr grins and glances at his partner, who suddenly gets the humor.

"We're not worried about a tape that's gonna burn up in two minutes."

"Just curious," I say, "as to what your story will be."

They come closer. This is getting uncomfortable. I hate crowds.

"We were driving by," he says with confidence, "heard some gunshots, and came rolling up here. The door was open, and we came in to find you on the patio. You'd shot the man inside in the back, then tried to kill Mrs. Jacobsen as she fled."

"For what purpose?"

"You figured out Louie killed Morrie Jacobsen, poisoned your dog, and broke into your house. When you ran into him here, you lost your head and shot him. Then when you found out he'd stolen a satchel full of cash, you decided you'd grab it, kill Mrs. Jacobsen, and head to South America."

"Wait a minute, Wahr. Then how'd I get this scratch on my arm?"

He glances around. "She tried to run away, you scuffled by the table, and the gun went off and hit you. Then you pushed her into the pool."

"Pretty lame. Anyway, what's my motivation?"

They just shake their heads. "Greed, plain and simple."

"Not in character for me."

"It's good enough for a jury. Besides, we're cops, no one will doubt our word. And Mrs. Jacobsen will back up our story, won't you, ma'am?"

Pale as a swan and dripping, she says, "I guess I'll have to."

"And how do you explain why you guys came out here and shot me?" I say.

"Easy. Mrs. Jacobsen was in the pool, and when we arrived, you'd just reloaded your revolver and were poised to kill her. When we yelled at you to stop, you shot at us, and we both returned fire."

"I suppose you're hoping I have extra ammunition."

"I can see the bullet pouch on your belt."

He's got me there.

"Any last words?" he asks, taking aim at my chest. What a cliché to die by. Damn.

Then I hear the most terrifying and yet sweetest sound on earth, that of a shotgun being racked: the metallic klack-klatch, as the action slides open, then slams shut, pumping a shell into the chamber.

"Drop those guns, you fucking punks," orders Detective Bagley.

Everyone looks over to the patio door.

Just like Bruce Willis, you gotta cheer him even when he delivers a standard line.

The bad guys lose their pieces and raise their hands. I start to cheer, inside my head, but then I catch the cold look in Wahr's eyes. With his hands raised, his coat standing open, I can see a pistol stuck in the front of his belt. Suddenly, he grabs for it and turns—

"Gun!" I shout, but I know it's too late. Before I realize it, I've grabbed the knife behind my neck. Wahr is ducked low and he's bringing up the pistol toward Bagley. I throw the knife hard and fast.

Bagley spots Wahr's movement and swings the shotgun toward him, but too late, as Wahr aims and . . . the double-edged knife sinks into the back of his shoulder and his body clenches hard, his head jerks, and he drops the gun, howls in pain, and clutches his arm.

Vickie looks wobbly, and I steady her.

Bagley steps over and kicks Wahr's pistol away, then orders both of the wayward cops to prone out on the deck.

"Jeff, that's the best entrance I've ever seen you make," I exclaim. "How'd you know to come here?"

He kneels down and cuffs the cops, then grunts as he stands up and says, "I just followed the smell these guys left behind when they bolted out of the station this morning. Had to figure they were up to something, I never saw them move so fast, not even to get donuts."

"They were the ones tailing me? I thought I lost them."

"It took them awhile, but they figured out you were here."

"Did you check their financial records?"

"Yep, and they have a lot of explaining to do. Of course, that's the least of their problems. Now they're facing conspiracy to murder."

The detectives have the longest faces I've ever seen on two grown men, not to mention that Wahr is still whining about his scratched shoulder. Haven't they ever heard that crime doesn't pay? Of course, neither does stargazing or PI work. Sirens are squealing in the background, and within a minute or so, two patrol cars screech to a stop outside. Ever vigilant.

I'm on my porch swing, swaying in a drowsy tempo. Binga's lying beside me on the hard boards. We're enjoying the fine fall day, and as I assess the case, I must admit there were some rewards in working it.

When I explained to Jeff Bagley about the two bags full of untraceable greenbacks, I could see his mental scales weighing options. His split would be over a million tax-free dollars and instant retirement, as against two more years of drudgery, likely risking his life, and receiving a modest pension at the conclusion.

I was glad to see integrity win the battle for his soul. And I learned that even great sums of money can't tempt me to abandon the life I've fashioned. I enjoy the fascination of nature, the company of a good dog, and the peace of mind to sleep well every night.

As I ponder my pleasurable but isolated existence, my thoughts drift to Amy Harrison. She was happy that I solved the case, even though her client didn't fare too well in the criminal justice arena. And she seemed truly concerned about my safety and well-being.

So this Saturday we'll be dining at a good restaurant, going over the details of my investigation, and, hopefully, getting better acquainted. I think I'd like to get to know her well. Time will tell.

Which leaves me with one more obligation in this matter. Picking up my cell phone, I call the Hillsboro FBI office. Jim answers again. Uncanny.

I tell him about the criminal enterprises springing up across the nation. "To put it in a metaphor," I say, "it's like the Mob is a black hole you can't see, but which powers all the activities in the crime universe. There are smaller galaxies in that universe, such as these crime centers they're building. Then you have stars, like our sun, represented by guys like Louie Minnelli."

"Are you saying Louie Minnelli was a major figure in this operation?"

"Put in perspective, astronomers call our sun a yellow dwarf."

He laughs, and says, "I'm not sure I follow all this astronomy gobbledygook, but I realize you're giving me the mother lode, crimewise."

"You deserve it. Work it, save our country, and get ready to be Director one day." Of course, he'll still have to battle it out with Marisol.

I hang up, feeling better. It's nice to find cheer in a situation in which I nearly got killed. But that's the true magic of our world: until we're smacked by a colossal comet, life on our planet goes on.

In one of his plays, Oscar Wilde wrote: "We are all in the gutter, but some of us are looking at the stars."

I can't think of anything I'd rather do.

About the Author

Mark Bouton was born and raised in Bartlesville, Oklahoma, and he majored in sociology at Oklahoma State University and earned a law degree at Oklahoma University. He's a life loyal member of the Sigma Chi fraternity. As an FBI agent for 30 years, he worked in Mobile, Alabama; New York; Washington, D.C.; Chicago; San Juan, Puerto Rico; Brownsville, Texas; San Antonio, Texas; and Topeka, Kansas. He arrested killers, kidnappers, and bank robbers and played a key role in solving the Oklahoma City bombing. Now retired from the FBI, he lives in Topeka, Kansas, where he does yoga, star-gazes, and writes mystery novels. Married, he has four boys. He's currently working on the second Max Austin novel in a series. Visit his web site at http://www.markbouton.com.

Web Sites of Interest:

Cosmic Sites:

http://science.nasa.gov/
http://www.astronomy.com/home.asp
http://www.space.com/
http://www.astronomyspace.com/
http://www.cosmic-concerns.net

Law Enforcement Sites:

http://www.fbi.gov/
http://www.interpol.com
http://www.copseek.com
http://www.officer.com
http://www.policescanner.com